Van Buren Denslow

Owned and Disowned

A Tale of Southern Life

Van Buren Denslow

Owned and Disowned
A Tale of Southern Life

ISBN/EAN: 9783337005238

Printed in Europe, USA, Canada, Australia, Japan

Cover: Foto ©Andreas Hilbeck / pixelio.de

More available books at **www.hansebooks.com**

OWNED AND DISOWNED;

OR,

THE CHATTEL CHILD.

Tale of Southern Life.

BY

VAN BUREN DENSLOW.

New-York:
H. DAYTON, 36 HOWARD STREET;
INDIANAPOLIS, IND.: ASHER & CO.
1860.

To

A DEVOTED WOMAN—A ZEALOUS CHRISTIAN,

AND A LOVED RELATIVE,

THE REVERED

MRS. SARAH G. BARKER,

OF HARTFORD,

THIS VOLUME IS RESPECTFULLY AND AFFECTIONATELY

DEDICATED,

BY HER NEPHEW,

THE AUTHOR.

PREFACE.

THE AUTHOR has endeavored, in the following pages, to weave into the narrative only such truthful and honorable sentiments as shall leave him no opportunity to regret the impressions it shall convey. The offspring of his thought, it has been to him rather a child than a chattel, and he would venture to hope that taking it with the hand of kindness, the reader, after perusal, will receive it as the same by adoption into the literary family which is ranged upon his shelf, to each member of which in turn he has been indebted for a pleasant and profitable hour. Great will he estimate his reward, if in addition, it shall contribute aught to the causes of social and spiritual freedom.

TABLE OF CONTENTS.

OWNED AND DISOWNED:

OR,

THE CHATTEL CHILD.

CHAPTER I.

THE TRAVELER.

" The winds came o'er his cheek, the soft winds blending
All summer sounds and odors in their sigh;
The orange-groves wav'd round, the hills were sending
Their bright streams down, the free birds darting by,
And the blue festal heavens above him bending,
As if to fold a world where none could die!
And who was he that looked upon these things?"

MRS. HEMANS.

" Look once again!   The moving canvass shows
A slave plantation's slovenly repose,
Where, in rude cabins, rotting midst their weeds,
The human chattel eats and sleeps and breeds;
And, held a brute, in practise as in law,
Becomes in fact the thing he's taken for."—WHITTIER.

THE sun was just sinking behind the rich tropical verdure, which, some forty years ago, lined and still continues to fringe, with agreeable, though somewhat monotonous sameness, the low bottom lands of the Mississippi River for a day's ride at least above New Orleans.

A single traveler, who had for a time been riding along in a careless revery, or occasionally reverting from the abstractions which occupied his mind, to glance at the broad lake-like river by whose banks he was riding, now picking up his thoughts and his reins together, studied for a moment a memorandum which he held, at the same time carefully scrutinizing the lonely scene around him, as if to compare it with the written instructions he had received, and pausing frequently as if doubtful of his way. Frequent paths branched off to the right, leading away from the river, into the dark groves or chapparells of cypress and cottonwood covered with festoons of moss. One of these courses he seemed desirous to take, but doubtful which to pursue, he submitted entirely to the energetic preferences of his little dapper mare, which jaunted forward with easy confidence until a turn in the river brought them to a clearing.

In the midst of the opening was a cluster of cabins. whose neatly white-washed fronts contrasted as singularly with the ebony forms now gathered in their doors and windows at the novel sight of a stranger, as their broad grinning countenances did with the whites and ivories they encircled. Around the cabins were some old, bent, white-headed negroes, who seemed to have out-lived the whole line of their posterity, and as if any future change in their aspect must certainly make them appear younger.   Upon the door-steps too, were women of all ages and shades of darkness, some wrinkled and homely enough to be hanged for veritable witches, having their heads bandaged with a coronet of flaming red handkerchiefs.   Whether these were used to prevent the smoke of their dirty clay pipes from escaping through any other than the proper vent, or from the fear that their artificial heat might crisp their natural head-dress into a tighter curl, and thus stretch their black skins into a still smoother and glossier tension, we must leave in doubt. Around their knees, in the windows and upon the sunny side of each cabin, were troops of shining little *oleagines*, in whose garb, as in their condition, the simplicity of nature was evidently but slightly marred.

A few small, shiftless vegetable gardens and the stumps of the cottonwood trees, which had been cut away to make the clearing and to build the cabins, completed the prospect.   Our traveler scrutinized the picture with some attention, as he approached the " quarters," and asked of a venerable old negro, if they belonged to Mr. Preston's plantation.

After repeating the question once or twice, he found the mumbling old patriarch had lost entirely too many of the five senses to comprehend it, and riding on, he addressed the same question to a younger mulatto, who advanced with the air of one consciously superior to his fellows, and with a negro's best imitation of the gentility of a Louisiana planter, said—

"Mass Preston reside in de family mansion ob de Prestons, 'bout half mile from dese ar quarters, an de gemmen no 'jections an will acquiesce to Alexander de great—hem—honor to 'scorch him from dis are to Lindenhall, he no fear ob transgression on de way."

As the stranger was disposed to restore to his pocket, with evident satisfaction, the written instructions by which most travelers in new countries, and, especially in the thinly settled parts of the Southern States, find it so difficult to chart out their way, and as he was equally pleased that as the negro seemed to express it, Alexander the Great should have the honor of preserving him from the sundry transgressions he might have been tempted to commit on the way, he consented to the service of the negro, and taking the path pointed out to him, rode on at a slow walk, and in a train of careless thought, until they had passed from the clearing. The slave attended closely but respectfully behind.

"How long has Mr. Preston resided here?" inquired the stranger, with a benevolent wish to give vent to the loquacity which was struggling for utterance in the negro.

" Oh, great many years, massa—great many years. Massa can hab no idea."

"Well, about how many ?" reiterated the traveler.

"Well," answered the negro slowly, pausing at each word, and stroking the fingers of his left hand with those of his right, as if entering into a labored calculation—"Well, massa, to de bes' ob my recollembrance, if I was to specify—'bout fifty years—massa. I am sartain sure it was summot not less than forty nor more than thirty, an I think de 'zact time was jes fifty. Massa—jes fifty years."

"How long have you been with him ?"

"Why, yah ! yah ! de Lor' sakes bless yer, massa, before he born—before eider of us was born. Did'n' my fader run all de little erran' for he fader an' mudder—poor deah sainted angel—God bless her—jes' to tink dat me know he mudder when he nebber know he ebber had a mudder if I did'n tell him—dat I should stan' by her bed, and see her lily angel face—whiter dan de whitest flower in de garden—an' her own chile neber climb her knee—neber kiss her—no, neber see her—poor tings—poor tings !" and the warm hearted negro who had begun his answer with a laugh ended it with a tear.

"Your master has spent his whole life here then ?" added the stranger after a pause.

"Oh ! no, massa ! he come here when he quite young man, from Ole Virginny. He quite a man den, an' he jis as young now, jis as handsome."

Perceiving from the negro's own age, which could not have passed forty, that the chronological information he had derived was of very doubtful value, the questioner concluded to direct him to topics better suited to his capacity.

"I understand you that neither of his parents are living."

"De livin' troof, massa. He mudder gabe him all her life, which wasn' much, poor ting—an' he fader follow her for de berry nex' funeral. So Massa Preston grow up heself—no fader, no mudder—jis bad off as poor little cotton-headed Sandy, when he stay in Virginny, an' he fader and mudder, bein only niggars, was sole off down to Georgy. Jis bad, poor tings. But de Lord take an' de Lord gib away, bressed be de Lord. Dat's what de min'ster said, and I beliebed it. So, bress de Lord, dars some consummation to trouble after all—an' dat ar's what I tell Massa Preston 'bout he own fader and mudder."

At the recurrence to these subjects, the simple negro plied his sleeve with a melancholy vigor to the corner of his left eye, and it was some time before his voice ceased to tremble with emotion.

"Mr. Preston has a family?" resumed the stranger.

Here the conversation was interrupted by the swift pattering of the hoofs of horses which were approaching them, accompanied by pleasant shouts and ringing laughter, which seemed to say as plainly as words could say it, that two young misses, just loosed from the fastidious shackles of a boarding-school, with enough of unspoiled nature to lead them into a roystering frolic, and with enough of cultivation to make it both a novel and mischievous method of killing time, were now spurring their fillys into a thorough boisterous race.

Our traveler had arrived at a fork in the roads, or rather paths, where, as his swarthy guide informed him, two avenues, crossing each other nearly at right angles, yet led, by about equally direct routes, to the mansion of Mr. Preston. One of these was lined by willows, whose long whips projecting, overhung the narrow road with their green curtains, so as to require no little temerity as well as steadiness in the saddle, to dash through them. Down this avenue came the two adventurous, rollicking riders, whose shouts they had heard, and who still, with their heads bent forward, and their colts pressed to their utmost speed, dashed forward in a style of boldness and off-hand grace, their loud laughter pealing forth like the rich songs of birds, the involuntary melody of enjoyment. So engrossed were they in the conscious enjoyment of such intense fun, that neither of them observed the presence of Sandy and the stranger until within a few feet of them.

The latter, as if unused to witness such feats, and not being certain but that the little steeds might have taken the contest too much into their own hands (or rather feet,) sprang quickly from his own horse, and would have intercepted that of the last rider ; but declining, with a smile, the proffered assistance, and waving her hand as she turned to him in passing, she showed him how little sense of danger she experienced, and probably how little there was, by a smart stroke upon the flanks with her little whip ; and in another moment the riders disappeared, and their more subdued laughter came ringing again through the twilight woods.

"Dat ar answers massa's question," said the negro, as they resumed their way. "Dat's our missuses—Miss July and Miss Ada. Poor Sandy nebber hab larnin' 'nuff to 'spatiate on dem ar. Dar's berry few as can 'spatiate on any subjec' like me. De angels, an' de debil, an' de garden ob Eden, an' de serpent wot undertook to swallow de big apple, an' de whale wot saved Jonah from de flood when de levee gub away down to New Orleans,—all dat ar I can 'spatiate on to good 'ceptance. But a live minister couldn't tell what dey are ; dey so good, so beautiful, so much heart for poor sufferin' niggers. Now, sez I to Aunt Tanzey, says I, ' I'm afeared de angels want

our missuses up dar,'" and Sandy pointed up into the
twilit sky.

"Dey change for de wos when dey make angels
   such like ; for de angels don't lub niggers. M
,rot a picture home ob de great judgment ob all
world before de big white throne ; an' der ain't a
single nigger in de picture 'cept one, an' dat's de debil.
An' de angels nebber weeps ; I see 'em true as natur
in a lubly little picture dat Miss Julia gub me wen
my little girl die ; an' de angels hab a little girl in
der arms carryin' her up troo de cloud ; but dey no
weep a tear. But wen I was sick ob de yaller fever,
Miss July come an' lean down ober poor nigger wen
he breff was p'ison, jes' as de angels lean ober de white
baby in de picture. Her big tear fall on my forehead,
an' I get well. An' Miss Ada come too, and lean
ober my Sally, an' look at her, an' de big tear fall on
her temples, right on de big black veins, an' 'mediate-
ly de fever break, an' she get well. An' wharsomeber
dey go on de whole plantation, no one die ; and dey
go eberywhere—so ebery body lib. An' if you don't
beleebe it, you can see dem all alibe and well when
you get up to de hall, and dat will prove every word
I say."

The stranger, smiling, intimated that he had not
the least doubt of his veracity, and Sandy, flattered
by his condescension, proceeded :

"But on ebery oder plantation dey all die. An' why didn't none die here ?· Kase ye see dey couldn't hab de heart to die, for bom-bye poor Miss July took sick as deff, and 'stead·o' her cheek look like roses, dey was jis' like—de Lor' forgive me—but dey was for all de worl' jis' like us poor niggas. An' den you s'pose we niggas lay down and tink ob our black, good for nuffin fever, as never was worf mindin' no how ! Do you s'pose dat ar, sir ?" and Sandy looked at the stranger suspiciously, as if the latter had accused him of picking his pocket.

"What did you do ?" inquired the stranger.

"Wot ! why, sa, no sooner we heard Miss July sick, dan we all jump up, sick an' well ; an' one ole man dat ebery body thought was dead long ago, jump up an' leff de quarters, an' run up to de hall, an' dar we stay weepin' an' cryin' an' runnin' ebery-where ; for dough we couldn't do any good, who could help doin' somefin.? An' so, before we knowed it, ebery body on de plantation seemed well but Miss July. But bom-bye we pray so loud, dat de Lord spare her ; he couldn't help it. I spec' he got putty tired hearin' us, an' concluded de plantation couldn't git along widout her. An' so now you see her, jis' as kind, an' good, an' beautiful as eber, an' jis' as much like angels, both of 'em, as dey could be, widout bein' not so good as dey am—'specially Miss July, and 'tic'-

larly Miss Ady. Ebery body worships dem, an' dey worships each oder."

" Do they live constantly at home ?"

" Oh, no, massa ; dey libs all around, eberywar—part de time here, an' part de time at Fifty-six, an' part de time at Concord-street, an' part at New Haven, an' part at Connecticut an' de New England States, an'—an' Concord-street, an' Connecticut, an'—an' all de oder big places 'twixt here and *thar*," said the negro, pointing upward. "I hopes dey won't move dar very soon. Dem am both jis' back from an emissary to de Norff."

" From a what ?" asked the traveler, amused.

"A large emissary, I tink, massa. But I'se no larnin', you know, 'sept my natural science, an' it was cither an emissary, or a ceremony, or a sight-o'-money. It was something that ladies have to get through with before deyse superfine, an' I'm not 'zackly sartin which."

" Don't you mean a seminary ?"

" Well, now, massa. Who'd a thought you'd a knowed de place better than Sandy ! But 'twas dat ar' 'zackly. Well, dar's nuffin' like larnin'—it kinder makes people know what dey don't know an' neber did. Now, I didn't know whether they had been to an emissary or a seminary, after bein' told, an' you knew all about it without. That's larnin'. Sez I to Aunt

Tanzey—sez I, 'Tanzey, brains and larnin' is vittels and drink.' Says she, 'Sandy, you fool, if it is how should you know it, for you never had any of it ?' an' sez I, 'Tanzey, de tings of de spirit am spiritually discerned.' "

Here Sandy paused to wipe off the perspiration engendered by his enthusiasm, and the traveler remarked—

"The ladies seem to pass their time very happily here."

"Oh, bery happy, bery. I hope de bright birds neber sing a sadder tune for de future to come dan dey have herebefore sung. All joy, all heaben wid dem ! I hope Miss Ada be happy, I know she will. I hope Miss July be happy, but Sandy 'fraid. Sandy be too wise. You know de Scripter somewhar says— 'de children of sinful generation,' which must mean de niggers, 'am wiser dan de children ob white folks.' I wish Sandy didn't know nuffin', den he wouldn' say, 'Good mornin', Miss July,' an' go away behind de crib an' sit he down an' cry for de two angels."

"Why do you cry for them ?" asked the traveler, adding, with assumed indifference, "mere whim, I suppose. Why do you pity Miss Julia more than Miss Ada ?"

"Oh, no reason 't all, massa—Sandy don't know nuffin' 'bout nobody, an' always did pity somebody as is not to be pitied. I know nuffin' 'bout Miss Julia. I hope she be berry happy."

Though the gentleman's interest in the conversation had much increased with the few last remarks, behind which he thought lay more meaning than the simple Sandy had intended to reveal, his attention was diverted from the conversation to the mansion of Mr. Preston, or, as it was styled, Lindenhall, which a turn in their path now brought to view.

It was a large, and rather antique and rusty-looking mansion, without architectural style, though superior in its commodiousness and air of wealth, to the majority of planters' residences. A spacious colonnade surrounded it on every side, and before it lay a wide meadow lawn, sloping down from the gentle rise upon which the mansion stood, till it reached the waters of the Mississippi, which, stretching out in broad and beautiful expanse, lent more than usual variety to the prospect from Lindenhall.

But while our traveler is thus surveying the prospect, let us take a closer view of him. Though rather above the medium height and size, and of a somewhat commanding presence, his smooth, almost beardless face indicates that he has seen but few of manhood's summers. His long, waving locks, fall in a sophomorical style over his shoulders. His eye is black, warm and passionate, and as he lifts his broad-rimmed palmetto, that his brows may be fanned by the cool evening air that comes sighing up from the river through the intermediate pines and cypresses, he exposes a countenance radiant with intellect and warmth—equally expressive of mildness and energy. Indeed, spite of a certain jaunty negligence in his dress and carriage, his open black eye and slightly contracted brows had a fixed expression of serene thoughtfulness, indicative of that deep enthusiasm of nature which must needs wear a veil of cloud over the burning geyser of its emotions, that such colder spirits as cannot appreciate may know nothing of its inward fires.

Having alighted at the Hall, and consigned his horse and a " fip" to the servant, he had no sooner set foot upon the steps of the colonnade, than the door opened, and a tall, well-formed, fashionably dressed man-of-the-world looking gentleman, with a keen grey eye, a smooth, whiskerless face, a fixed and changeless smile, and a low, soft, seductive voice, which involuntarily suggested to the mind the quiet rustle of grass through which a serpent is moving, said—

" Why, my dear old friend, if you had not been true to the appointed time, I should not have recognized you. Believe me, my dear Captain, I am most happy to see you. I see you look astonished—no doubt I have changed much more than yourself. Why, you look younger than you did twelve years ago,—but walk in, sir."

Our traveler, with an involuntary air of surprise, was about to reply to this hurried tirade—

"I beg pardon, sir—I am no Captain, but simple *Mr.* Defoe"——

"Oh, certainly, sir," said Preston, in a whisper, interrupting him. "Excuse my indiscretion. I admit that we ought, in a matter of this kind, for it is," and here his whisper sunk so as to be nearly inaudible, "it is, to say the least of it, diabolical. We cannot be too discreet; but walk in, sir."

With this, Defoe returned the studied bow and equally studied pressure of the hand, and entered the hall. The expression of surprise at his reception had vanished from his countenance, but a scrutinizing observer might have perceived that he kept upon his host, for some reason, an intensely interested and watchful eye; as the latter continued the conversation in the same rapid though stealthy and half inaudible manner.

"You shall see your game soon—a perfect charm—believe me, a *fetisha.* You'll be entranced beyond measure. But she is yours. Pity I can do nothing better for her. I pity her as a father should. Step into the library. There now we are secure from being overheard. So is fate. So we're born, you know."

"Yes," replied the stranger. "'There is a providence which shapes our ends, rough hew them as we will.' "

"Ha! ha! Admirable. You will succeed—no doubt of it. Take that rocking chair, do, my dear friend.   Ah, that hair of yours is a *chef d' ouvre* in the art of disguise.   D—— my soul if it isn't, and your face, the smoothest cheek certainly in your profession. Why, you look as much like a northern freshman, as the day we ran away from Yale twelve years ago.   By the way, hadn't you better appear in that character ?"

"I think I had," replied Defoe.

"Admirable—and your name.   What shall that be ? Something sounding and *distinguè*. Say De La Fontaine—heir to an immense estate in the south of France.   Or what think you of Fitz Gerald ?   Say Fitzmaurice Fitz Gerald, Esq., eldest son of the Earl of Fitz What-d'ye-call-em.   Women are devilish easy taken by the Fitz, you know.   What shall your name be ?"

"Defoe."

"Devil !   Why use your real name ?"

"Why any other ?"

"Why ! hath your right hand forgot its cunning ? I will tell you why.   You must probably go into society.   Julia has seen something of the world, and may prove a siege.   For mind you, nothing shall be done without her consent.   Now nothing fritters away a woman's moral stubbornness so quick as fashionable life—balls—suppers—theatres—and how many of these could you visit in New Orleans without being unpleasantly recognized as Lieutenant Defoe of the 'Flying Scud ?' "

"And then I perceive," suggested Defoe, "the game with me and my flash brothers of the skull and crossbones would be up."

" Precisely ! and instead of the noose of love, your neck would find a noose of hemp ! Confide not too much in past good fortune."

Defoe mused thoughtfully for a moment, and then said—

" I see the force of your objection. I think, however, I will still preserve the name of Defoe. I have a lickspittle brother at the North, whom, as I have heard, she met and remembers with kindness, and this, perchance, may be of advantage to me."

" Indeed !"

" Besides, I have lately traveled in nearly every city of the South, and there is not the slightest danger of my being taken for the interesting young pirate of Barrataria. Trust to me. Honor among thieves, you know—ha ! ha ! Preston."

"Ah ! yes," said Preston, drily. "Ha ! ha ! I didn't see the point at first, but—ha ! ha ! that was always your motto.   Here's my hand upon it, Captain Defoe."

"Mr."

"Beg pardon, *Mr.* Defoe ; of what college ?"

"Yale."

"Sure enough !   Yale college, of course—ha ! ha !" continued Mr. Preston, laughing.   Defoe also laughed with apparent heartiness.

But as the two gentlemen sat eyeing each other for a few moments afterward in silence, it was well for each that the shadows of evening twilight concealed the expression which sat upon the countenance of the other.   As the wealthy planter rose to ring for a servant, the light of the harvest moon fell full upon his countenance, which seemed to the calm but earnest scrutiny of Defoe to wear the diabolical malignancy of a fiendish heart—daring only under cover of the twilight to withdraw that veil of smiles, behind which it lay like a beast of prey in ambush.

CHAPTER II.

MODERN CHIVALRY.

" Full of those dreams of good that, vainly grand,
Haunt the young heart,—proud views of human kind,
Of men to Gods exalted and refined,—
False views, like that horizon's fair deceit,
Where earth and heaven but *secm*, alas, to meet!"
MOORE's "*Lalla Rookh.*"

WALTER DEFOE had been among the most earnest, enthusiastic, and ambitious students at Yale College. He had been reared, or rather he had reared himself, amidst the high-toned religious influences of a small Puritan village in the neighborhood, for the early death of his father had left his intelligent and pious, but invalid mother entirely dependent upon him for support. Mrs. Defoe had been the mother of two children—Conrad, the eldest of whom, Walter dimly remembered among the other associations of his infancy as a handsome and gallant, but wild and impetuous young man. The charity of his parish had afforded to him a term in college ; but disgracing their charity, he had been dismissed from college, and after having done much to injure the health and wound the heart of his affectionate parent, finally went to sea. Since then no better tidings had been received from him than might have been expected from his youthful-career ; and the absence of all intelligence of him for many years, had finally confirmed his friends in the belief that he was dead.

With a beauty of filial affection which won the hearts of all who knew him, and by the incessant, but feeble struggles by which youthful weakness finds it so difficult to support itself, and still more another dependent person, Walter sought to support and make happy his mother's destined path of premature decline.

He went into the hot, steaming factory when he had to mount a stool to reach up to the work of the other boys, and there toiled on from early dawn to dusky twilight, till his little round red cheeks grew thin and pale, and the bones began to show themselves in sharp lines upon his face, just as they did upon his mother's. Still he toiled on, for his mother day by day was dying. And though sometimes when he stopped on his way to work, and peered between the bars of the great iron fence around the lawns and parks, and saw the rich people and their children enjoying the bright day, the healthy air, and the green grass and blossoming trees, and thought what a fine place this world must be for them, and how, if he should live to be a man of wealth, he would go about

doing good, and especially would endeavor to save
little children everywhere from having such a hard
life as he had, which made him feel often as if he
could not help stealing something, no matter what—
when I say he thought of these things, he would
sometimes wish, on his way home, that he might not
be obliged to work in the hot, steaming factory, in
which he must die in two or three years, but that he
might find some healthier employment, in which he
could live to manhood.

But when he took his little earnings on Saturday
night and spent them all for tea, preserves, and medi-
cines for his mother, and the simplest food for both
of them, and when his poor sick mother would curl
up his little feet under him like the Turk in the picture books, and have him sit down beside her upon
the bed where she had lain for so long a time, and
talked to him about the dangers which would beset
him when he should enter the world as a man, how
hard it would be for him to keep himself unspotted
from the world, and how fondly she hoped he would
live and die as pure as he then was, and so would
come to her in heaven, then little Walter would fall
upon his mother's neck and cry ; and though he would
not tell her so, he would thank God that the hot, un-
healthy factory would hasten his flight home to his
dear, dear mother in heaven. Then for mornings

after, when he went to his work, he would not loiter
by the great park where happy children frolicked, but
would steal around by the cemetery, and peeping between the pickets, would think of the time when those
willows would weep and those cypresses sweetly moan
over the green, pretty graves of his mother and himself, and their souls should have been taken by the
Lord as a mother folds her child to her bosom.

But through the darkest clouds some cheering rays
of light will steal.

Deserted by her old friends, sick, poor, and without
hope, with no prospect but of destitution before her,
chance, or the unseen influence of angels of mercy, had
directed to her threshold one of those gentle creatures
whose mission on earth is to love and to bless—not
one of those meteoric fashionables which glare up
with a train of sparks behind them, and having excited
the admiration of fools, who do not know that they
are nothing but a fizzle of powder and wadding, which
any Chinaman can make, then disappear just this side
of heaven, and fall forgotten before they reach the
ground—but one of those lovely stars most admired
by loftiest minds, which illumine the darkness of poverty and despair, ever guiding the erring, and attract-
ing the eyes of all to purity and heaven.

Younger even than Walter, this little girl, with
rich, pouting lips, and dark brunette complexion, jet

black ringlets, and large sparkling eyes of an irresistibly melting softness and lustre, appeared to him like an etherial vision in a dream. But the tasteful elegance of her āttire, contrasting with the tattered garments over his own squalid form, reminded him painfully of this world of unequal realities, and of his own inferior station.

What first brought her to their threshold they knew not, but no sooner had she left than by indirect means, which she delicately resorted to in order to divert their attention from her as the donor, every comfort of life was constantly supplied to them. With her own hands she would sometimes bring a bit of jelly, or a bouquet of flowers, or other delicate little attention for the sick woman, or sitting down by her bed-side, during long hours when Walter was obliged to be at the factory, from her own lips she would read with melodious beauty of voice and accent whatever she thought would be most soothing and consoling to a sensitive, sick, destitute and dying widow and mother.

Thus had she visited them for months, nor had the little creature revealed herself to them by any other name than that by which she fondly insisted upon being known—of "daughter" to the widow, and "sister" to the orphan who were the recipients of her bounty.

At last, one day after his mother had been more ill

for several days than usual, while little Walter was working in the factory, and so weak that he could scarcely lift the light implements of his dull, monotonous task, suddenly the machinery began to quiver and tremble, as if the building was falling, and the poor, sick child, shrieking the name of his mother, sank to the floor.   Weeks passed, and Walter did not return to the factory, nor did his little hands toil there more, for he lay tossed with a fever under the care and nursing of a kind old Quakeress.   Sometimes he was so feeble he would utter no sound for days, and sometimes he was strong enough to converse with his mother, and with the kind little girl whom he called his "sister." He talked with them about the trees and flowers in the park, and about the pretty, neatly dressed little boys and girls, and would often smile and laugh, and the time passed pleasantly.

But no mother, and, after the first few days of his sickness, no sister conversed with him, save in the fancies of his delirium.   It was not, however, until he was quite strong and well, that in answer to his continued inquiries for his mother, the kind old Quaker lady told him that she was no more, and that the little girl who used to visit her in her sickness, had been obliged to return a long way off to her home, so that Walter could not even render one word of thanks to the beautiful young stranger for whom he could not but feel the most intense admiration and gratitude. But the good are never forgotten. Her sweet image, like a guardian spirit, had been with him in his dreams, and had guided and inspired his life with a mysterious but hallowed influence. Delusive hope it may have been, yet oh, how fondly the struggling youth cherished it, how it encouraged him through "long days of labor and nights devoid of ease," that at some of the turnings of life, that sweet smile, that kind eye, would again rest, if but for a moment, on him.

As soon as he had recovered, he left the " Orphan's Home," of which the old Quakeress was but the matron, and went out and looked up and down the street, and felt for the first time that he was utterly alone in the world. Need we recount the long years of menial struggles by which the lonely orphan worked his way upward from indigence and despair to a position of comparative ease. Need we say with what conscious pride he entered, by means of the proceeds of his own labors, the very college from which his brother had been ignominiously expelled, or with what assiduity he had there prosecuted his studies.

Though he had not yet chosen what profession he should pursue, the generous instincts of his heart and the influence of his revered mother, made him recoil from the pursuits of selfishness, and caused him to struggle for some position in which he might live a

life of enlarged usefulness, and he had a noble ambi-
tion to be useful in alleviating, to some extent, those
social inequalities and evils against some of which he
had struggled, and which blight the happiness of the
majority of mankind.

Such were the day-dreams of the studious youth,
which, with another and more tender fancy that sometimes floated pleasantly before his mind, encouraged
him onward.   When, one morning as he was passing
the celebrated seminary of the Misses Willis, the steps
of which a bevy of young ladies were at the moment
ascending, one of them strangely riveted his attention.
Her complexion, darker even than that which usually
obtains under Italian skies, was tinged so delicately
that an artist might have studied its hues entranced.
Her lips, faultless in form, were of ruby richness, and
her exuberant folds of raven hair fell around her finely
chisseled neck with a

" Grace beyoud the reach of art."

But more than all, her softly intellectual forehead, beneath which shone the deep fond light of a benevolent,
yet languishing and passionate eye, might have persuaded the student that he had strayed into the society of an angel, did not her finely moulded and volup-
tuously graceful form recall everything most beautiful
in woman.   As she went tripping up the· long flight
of steps, she turned. and her eye rested intently upon

that of the student.   Did they recognize each other, or had they ever met before ? for each marked the flush upon the cheek of the other.

Back upon Walter's mind, like the rush of a spring flood, came hurried thoughts of past years, of the old Quakeress, of the factory, of his invalid mother, and finally her angel nurse.

" Is it—can it be her ?" the student half exclaimed, as he turned to take one more look at that inexpressibly fascinating countenance.   But the vision had vanished, the door had closed, and he wended once more upon his way, musing and—in love.

A week of delightful imaginations determined his resolution ; and notwithstanding the environing obstacles with which the vigilance of most principals guards the ladies in their seminaries from the formation of new acquaintances, another week of industry and address sufficed to place Defoe upon calling terms at the establishment of Miss Willis, where he found that the Misses Preston—one of whom was the benefactor of his infancy and of his mother's widowhood—had departed finally for their home, which was the residence of a planter in the vicinity of New Orleans, where, or whether ten or a hundred miles distant, he could not learn.

Six months wore away, and Walter Defoe, though in the apparent effort industrious, was in reality absent, idle, and dreamy.   At the end of this time, and a few months before the opening of our narrative, he disappeared from college, and not being heard from for some time, nor responding to the anxious inquiries made for him, as usual in such cases, such of his friends as were worth having preserved their faith in his worth undimmed, while those who were not shook their heads, and said they had always thought it strange that any brother to Conrad Defoe could sincerely be as gentle and good a person as Walter seemed.   They hoped so ; but they had their doubts.   And while they were eagerly and suspiciously doubting, young Walter Defoe had searched for, and at last found, the roof which sheltered Julia Preston, and where, by some remarkable coincidence, the cause or nature of which he darkly suspected, but had not yet unraveled, he found himself a thrice welcome guest, but welcome on account of some assumed character which had been unexpectedly thrust upon him, but which he, with prompt and almost instinctive foresight, had determined to wear as best he could, until it should reveal to him somewhat more clearly the character of his remarkable host, so strangely shadowed forth in the manner of his reception.

"Julia and Ada, it affords me much pleasure," said Mr. Preston to his daughters, at a later hour of the evening in which the incidents of the former chapter occurred, " to introduce to you a young man, yet of long and dear acquaintance, the son of my old and well-remembered friend, Mr. Defoe, of Virginia. I commend him to your kindest hospitality, and hope he will not regret having honored Lindenhall with his presence, nor be found sighing too soon for the classic precincts of Yale.

CHAPTER III.

THE COVENANT.

" Together, 'neath the early morn,
    We took our joyous way,
When clustering blossoms hid the thorn,
    And all around was gay.

And now, when midnight's wildest storms
    The troubled sleeper wake,
And fear unveils its phantom form,
    Shall I thy side forsake?"   MRS. SIGOURNEY.

IT was after midnight, and but a single glimmeri
taper told of life within Lindenhall. Near to this,
and before a large mirror, each gazing at the reflected
features of each other, stood Julia and Ada Preston.
Their arms fondly enfolded each other in a sisterly
embrace, and they seemed to twine together as vine
around vine, when it has no other supporting prop.
Their temples fondly met and pressed each other, and
Julia's luxuriant curls of glistening jet mingling with
Ada's waving locks of light auburn, fell upon their
shoulders as they stood

" Side by side, * * *
In rosy dream, hand interlocked in hand,
And clustering curls commingled."

The voluptuous loveliness of the creole, mingling, perhaps, with the pride of the Spanish and the grace of the French, combined in Julia with the mentality of the American ; while Ada's golden hair, and pale, slightly tinged cheek, blue eye, and slender, fairy form shone with the pearl-like fairness of the Saxon. But there was in her delicate and childish features an infantile prettiness, which contrasted with the dignified intellectuality of her sister, and compared with her, she seemed like a doll-like, though lovely creature, whom no years could change from child to woman. Such doubtless are sent to earth like flowers and cloud-tints, only to gratify our taste and love for the beautiful and pure. Julia had changed little since she last arrested the eye of the New Haven student, save that the few intervening months may have added a richness to the rose upon her cheek which the brown complexion she had derived from her Southern birth and parentage could not hide, or may have perfected the graceful contour of womanhood in a form which seemed the fit temple of all that was pure and affectionate in woman's nature.

" Ah, Julia," said Ada, smiling, " I knew you would never love where there was no romance. Don't smile and shake your head and say, ' No, sister, I love none but you,' for it won't do. That doesn't solve the

mystery.   Now, isn't there a mystery about this matter, sister Julia ?"

"Certainly, it looks quite mysterious, but——"

"Don't say 'but,' Julia—say it's a mystery, and
stop. Oh, I like mysteries. If ever I fall in love, it
will be with some one I never have seen nor heard of,
and don't know anything about, just for the sake of
the mystery.   Wouldn't that be interesting ?"

"I should think it would be decidedly interesting,"
said Julia, laughing.

"Well, this is just such a mystery exactly !   Here
you have hardly ever seen him or heard of him, and
of course you can know little about him.   Is not the
case precisely parallel ?"

"Except that my pretty sister's imagination only
has supplied the fact that I am already in love with
him, which, you must know, is very presumptuous
and absurd."

"No matter how presumptuous' or absurd it is
since you have frankly admitted it to be a fact," replied Ada, archly.   "Now, sister, put your lips close
to mine—there, not yet—now. I want you to kiss
me—if you think you are in love, if not, don't. There,
I thought you would. Now, you see, I've found it
all out, and I am very sorry for it, very sorry."

"Why would you be sorry, if you should find any
such fancy as you now entertain to be true, dear Ada ?"

"Oh ! there's something so horrid in the idea of loving men. I don't see how girls that have any kind of respect for themselves can do it. I am sure I never could. They're all such rude, ungraceful savages. When I fall in love, it'll be with a woman—there ! There's something kind and tender and gentle about you. I wish I were a man, so that you could love me more than a sister. A love deeper than ours would seem so strange. The pilgrimage of this romantic student to the shrine of his lady love would be nothing compared with my knight errantry."

"Sister Ada thinks men are demons, whom it is impossible to love, and yet wishes herself were one of those demons."

"Oh, you are always cross-examining," replied Ada.

"I don't mean that exactly—I only mean that I shall be very sorry when you come to love any other person more than Ada, and when you will leave all others, including Ada, to cleave to that one. Then we who have gathered nothing but flowers in the path of life so pleasantly shall be separated. You shall take one path and I another, and we shall not see each other for months, who knows but years ! Oh, it would be so sad   Why can we not love each other only and always until we die ? I should ask no other happiness. A fig for marriage. I wish we were two old maids now, so homely that nobody would want to marry either of us.   I should be perfectly happy.   I tell you I am going to be an old maid.   I should like to see some great monster ask me to love him.   I should like to be a vestal virgin, or a nun, or something, but to be loved.   Oh, it must be horrid.   Dear me !"

"I fear pretty sister Ada must soon fall upon some very terrible experiences unless she screens her person as well from all mankind as she has hitherto retained her heart," said Julia, kissing her.

"I have no fear of that," said Ada, "for I shall not be pretty after a couple of years, but shall grow to a very plain girl, and if I can only stand it the couple of years, after that I shall 'not be tempted, neither tempt any man'—so you see I am almost an old maid now."

"Well, by a hard struggle, I think you may continue to be," said Julia, laughing, "but come, can't you solve this mystery ?"

"It is very strange," whispered Ada, "that the awkward, bashful student, whose wits you frightened out of his head, at New Haven, should have taken this quixotic journey, or should have found business which should bring him here."

"And still more strange," pursued Julia, "that he should have met with such a cordial reception from pa !"

"Wonderful!" repeated Ada, in an emphatic whisper. Besides we learned in New Haven that he was a poor orphan who had supported himself by the vilest occupations until he had risen to his present position, and yet pa told us he was the son of a wealthy friend of his in Virginia, now living, and the heir at his father's death to immense wealth."

"Pa appears to take much interest in him, and is very anxious indeed that we should be pleased with him," continued Julia.

"Or rather that you should," laughed Ada.

"I cannot conceive how or why pa should have conceived anything particular relative to the matter."

"Oh, sister, I feel a strange presentiment that we are some way to be separated. Our hours of joyous companionship together are fading away, even now, like the beauty of the clouds at sunset. A dark cloud obscures our future, and I cannot penetrate it ; but, dear sister, whatever may befal either of us, will you, to your dying day, when you think of your poor sister Ada, say, " Poor child, she did not mean to do wrong !"

Julia was too much accustomed to the child-like waywardness of her sister to be much surprised by her sudden and melancholy forebodings, and only replied,

" Yes, child, but do not be sad."

And as the streaks of morning light shone through

the lattice, the sisters sealed the covenant of endless affection with a kiss, and flinging themselves down upon a couch, they folded each other in a still closer embrace, and wept themselves to sleep.

CHAPTER IV.

BETROTHED.

" Ah, happy love ! where love like this is found ;
  Oh, heartfelt raptures ! bliss beyond compare !
I've paced much this weary, mortal round,
  And sage experience bids me this declare—
If heaven a draught of heavenly pleasure spare,
  One cordial in this melancholy vale,
'Tis when a youthful, loving, modest pair,
  In other's arms breathe out the tender tale
Beneath the milk-white thorn, that scents the evening gale."
Burns.

A week had nearly passed, and not unpleasantly, apparently, to the inmates of Lindenhall, since the arrival of Walter Defoe.   The mornings were occupied by rides upon horseback along the romantic paths that skirted the banks of the river, occasionally relieved by a pleasant sail upon its own broad current.   The short afternoons passed swiftly away in the perusal or discussion of the merits of favorite authors, and other subjects of a literary, poetical, or pleasing interest, in which the rarely cultivated mind of the student delighted to revel.   Here, indeed, his richly stored intellect appeared to the best advantage, and his earnest

2

efforts to please were rendered still more certainly successful by the consciousness that in one, at least, of his audience, he found a tender and sympathetic appreciation.

But it was especially delightful to the young student to sit by the open window, or upon the long piazza, and receive the gentle, refreshing influence of the cool zephyrs of evening, while one or the other of the sisters would cast a lulling, happy influence over his soul by singing some plaintive or thoughtful melody, occasionally accompanied by the piano or guitar, a melody often that would recall his mother's sweet voice, or remind him of the bitter hours of his childhood. Sometimes, however, it would touch upon happier themes, and stir his soul to warmer and more genial thoughts. At such moments he would look out into the future in a half bewildered but beautiful dream, in which he was surrounded by associations and affections and beings who seemed thrown around him as if by a providential love, desirous to make the perfect bliss of his future life a contrast to the hard struggles of the portion he had passed through.

These amusements Mr. Preston appeared to have leisure only occasionally to favor with his encouraging presence. But the labors and cares of superintending his extensive plantation, one of the largest in the State of Mississippi, was, and indeed seemed to have always served with his daughters as a sufficient excuse for his almost constant absence from the society of his house, either upon his plantation or in New Orleans. The happy hours of those few days had not been listlessly passed by the New Haven student. With Julia he had talked, walked, rode, sailed, played and sung, and every moment added fresh evidence to him that the external grace which had first drawn his attention was but the fit shrine of the pure and lovely qualities which had so soon after won his heart. As they communed more and more together, there grew up rapidly between them a fitness of thought and a congeniality of soul, which seemed to open upon one of them like a new world, while the heart of the other was borne along as in a current, without herself realizing the truth, or certainly much more rapidly than she would have confessed it. Julia had seen much of society, where her charms had brought her many admirers—and she had come to think the day far distant when, with all her affectionate kind-heartedness, her womanly vanity would not be better pleased to be the centre of the admiration of many than to be the exclusive possession of one. But she could not fail to see young Walter's meaning, and notwithstanding the contradictory and mysterious circumstances of his coming, it would have been somewhat strange, as Ada hinted, had she failed to have been pleased by it.

It was at the close of a day which had passed like a delightful trance, in some of the amusements we have mentioned, that Walter and Julia were seated upon a rustic couch at the foot of a branching willow by the margin of the river.

The evening had been warm, but now the gentle zephyrs moved refreshingly through the dewy foliage around them, and the moon glistened over the still expanse of waters which stretched out in placid beauty at their feet.

At the request of Julia, Walter had narrated his whole early life, had depicted the wrongs and sting of his early poverty, the story of which, up to the death of his mother, she had long since known. Since that time he had wandered, without a relative, without a home, but such as his own often unsuccessful labors provided for him, without friendship or any human heart to whom he could look for encouragement or love, cheered only by the vision of one never absent from his mind, never forgotten, who had been the foster-daughter to his dying mother and the guardian angel of her orphan son.

With a fluency which was kindled into eloquence by the sympathy of his listener, he recounted the various steps of triumph or defeat in his school, mercantile, and college life, up to the moment he had again seen her, and then with blushing cheek and quivering lip he spoke of a few months of dreamy college life, in which his books were neglected and his honors lost, then of his departure from college, his arrival at New Orleans, his various endeavors in a search in which he had scarcely a clue to his success, his repeated disheartening failures, and his final partial success.

At the word " partial" the delicate hand which rested in his own tenderly returned its thrilling pressure, and a single dewy drop from the downcast eye of the maiden fell and glistened upon it.   He stooped to brush it with his lips away, and as he did so their attention was arrested by a dark figure moving stealthily along the path from which they had stepped aside to the rustic couch.   Walter started towards it, but upon a nearer approach it seemed to resolve itself into a young cypress tree, stirred by the gentle motion of the evening winds.   Taking Julia's arm within his own, slowly and pausing often to lengthen out in trembling but ill-disguised confessions the rapturous moments which both felt, as if they would fain retain and expand if possible into ages, they returned to Lindenhall !

CHAPTER V.

THE "PECULIAR INSTITUTION."

" Unchristian thought ! on what pretence soe'er
Of right inherited, or else acquired ;
Of loss, or profit, or what plea you name,
To buy and sell, to barter, whip, and hold
In chains a being of celestial make—
Of kindred form, of kindred faculties,
Of kindred feelings, passions, thoughts, desires-
Born free, and heir of an immortal hope !
Thought villainous, absurd, detestable !
Unworthy to be harbored in a fiend."
POLLOK's " Course of Time."

SCARCELY had they reached the threshold, when the door was opened, and Ada appeared, so pale and agitated that her sister, flying to her arms, exclaimed :

" Dearest Ada, what is the matter ?   Are you sick ? Speak, sister !"

" No," whispered Ada, laying her hand upon her heart, as if to still its painful beatings—"I am not sick ; but—oh, come with me !"

Ada threw her arms around her sister, who was in a tremor of agitation, and pale herself in her deep sympathy for the suffering girl, and kissed her, as if she feared she would soon be deprived of that oppor-

tunity, and repeating hurriedly, " Come with me,"
she glided into the hall, and bounded up the stairs.

" Mr. Defoe, will you excuse me for a moment ? I
fear my sister is quite unwell," whispered Julia. " I
see my father waiting in the library. I am sure he
would like your company, which his business of late
has left him so little opportunity of enjoying."

" Certainly," said Walter.

And as the maiden tripped lightly up stairs to join
Ada, she heard Mr. Defoe enter the library, and receive the same cordial greeting which had, from his
first arrival, seemed so remarkable, but which now
appeared to her only as one of a chain of circumstances
providentially linked together for *their* happiness.

Upon entering her sister's room, she found Ada still
pale and agitated, kneeling before a small silver crucifix, with her hands clasped, her sweet blue eyes, full
of devotion, lifted upward in the posture of prayer.—
Never, she thought, had Ada appeared so lovely, as
kneeling now in woman's most graceful attitude—not
indeed as revealing most grace of limb or of outward
form, but of heart. Julia paused in awe for a moment,
and then silently approaching, yielded to the power
of sympathy, and knelt by her side.

In a moment, Ada, turning with a tearless face,
though quivering with convulsive emotion, took the
hands of Julia in hers, and covering with them her

own face, as if to hide from her sight the effect of her words upon her sister, said :

"Julia, Julia ! prepare to be overwhelmed by an affliction such as you can neither avoid nor bear, that makes me doubt even while I pray. Oh, Julia, if angels ever weep, all heaven is weeping for you now ! Oh, if it is so hard to tell the story, how can you hear it ! O God ! help us both." And as she said this, the fountain of her tears burst forth, and hiding her face in the bosom of her sister, she wept, convulsively.

"God will help us, love," said Julia, calmly. "Pray, calm yourself, and do not fear but that I can bear what you have heard. What is this danger of which you cannot speak, and which affects me more than yourself, or than our dear father, or from which he cannot protect ?"

"He protect ! Oh, Julia, you have no father. Would I had almost said that I had none !"

"Ada !"

"He whom you call your father is the father only of your shame. Nay, he has sold you, as he would a common negro, to yonder wretch, outlaw, pirate, fiend, Defoe, who is even now bantering with him about the price. Oh, sister,' tis true !" she cried, embracing the trembling Julia, who gazed upon her in incredulous, speechless consternation.

"Sold me—his daughter !"

"You ! his—his—Oh, sister of my soul ! mother of all that is good in me ! you are indeed his child, but his—his—I cannot say it."

Julia, growing paler and paler as her sister had proceeded, now stood with cheek of livid whiteness, with eyes uplifted, as if her mind were wandering through the dim mazes of some fearful dream. Not a tear coursed down her cheeks, or even moistened her brilliant, flashing eye. Withdrawing herself from Ada's embrace, she turned and gazed earnestly upon her reflected likeness in the nearest mirror, as if to read there the hard story which her sister could not tell. Unloosing her hair from her comb, she brought her long jetty curls before her shoulders, until they covered her whole bosom, and fell down below her waist.

They were exuberant and beautiful, and her pride had often looked upon those waving raven folds with womanly delight. As she drew away her hand, she held that off, and scanned its pallid whiteness. Then her gaze wandered from feature to feature of her countenance, till at last it vibrated between her own rich ruby lips and black, lustrous, and passionate eye. At length her lips moved, and murmured in a low, distant voice, as if her soul had been spirited away, and was speaking from afar off—

"Julia—Julia is a slave ! I am Julia ; I am a slave ; poor slave !"

This delirious calmness lasted but for a moment ; then her proud form rose to its full and beautiful stature. She seemed in an exultant trance, then as if it were the sound of the spirit of liberty vacating the chambers of her soul for the demon of slavery to enter, throwing up her arms, her pent-up passions burst forth, half whispering, half shrieking—

"No, I am free !"

But slowly returning to her former attitude, again ever and anon muttered,

"No ! no ! I am a slave—a slave !"

Suddenly arousing from her lethargy, she shrieked with a fearful vehemence—

"Prove this. Prove it. Quick, Ada, for the air of slavery is the air of hell ! It stifles me, and I can breathe it no longer. If I am a slave, let me know it that I may die and be free !"

As she said this, a form which she had not recognized before, and which, at any other moment, would have startled her, but to which she now calmly looked as the natural response to her enquiry, arose from his seat in a shadowed corner of the room, and came forth where the light of the single lamp fell upon his features. His bald and venerable head, white neck-band and priestly cassock, but above all, his reverend and holy mien, filled her with instant confidence, and falling down before the holy father, with her cross to her lips, she besought his blessing and his aid.

" The former I give you now," said he, blessing her. " The latter I have come to give you if I can."

Then raising her up, he continued—

" Daughter, in the secrecy of the confessional chamber, I have learned of the villainy which plots your destruction, from the very pirate and fiend who this night kissed your hand under the branches of the willow by the river. I knew your mother well. She was beautiful and accomplished, virtuous and pious, but a quadroon, and the property of Mr. Preston. Her father and owner had intended to free her, but died suddenly, and she was thrown into the market for sale. Young Preston, impressed by her mental and moral superiority, purchased her through an agent, and did not even permit her to know that he was her owner, but visiting her as a friend, with honeyed words upon his lips, proposed to secure her liberty and make her his wife. So he gained her affections, and she yielded to her lover and affianced husband, what as her owner even he would blush to have enforced. It was not until after your birth, that he received the title papers for yourself and mother. Accident has placed them in my hands. You may read them," said the priest, producing a soiled, worn paper, and carefully unfolding it, lest it should fall to pieces in being opened.

Julia glanced over the paper hurriedly. Having acted often as her father's secretary in engrossing and arranging many papers of the same nature, it was not difficult for her to judge of its genuineness or import. It was the bill of sale of her body and soul. Attached to it as subscribing witness was the single name which thrilled her to her very heart—" Defoe !"

" Shortly after your birth," continued the priest, " your mother was at the same time, by the small-pox, deprived of her beauty and freed from her slavery, but repentance and anguish wrought so powerfully upon her mind, and the sins which she saw in a life in which others saw only misfortunes, induced her to seek a refuge in the arms of the church and in the holy order of mercy, from the pollution of the world. But in taking the vail, she did not banish from her heart her love for her child, and though you have not known it, her prayers and her watchfulness have ever attended you."

" Yes," said Julia. " Holy father—I see it and believe it all. It is hard. It stuns me. I am blinded and bewildered. I hoped at first this dream would break, and I awaking would clasp my pillow in my frenzied hands as I have often done when some horrid vision of the night had passed, and smile to think it was all false. But no. I see it all now. It is all true. My thanks, reverend father, for the kind manner in which you have performed this task, for I suppose my master—Oh, God!" exclaimed the stricken girl, as she clasped her throbbing brows in anguish at the utterance of that word—"I suppose my owner has bid you break this fearful news to his chattel child. Go then and tell him—him whom my best nature hath always taught me to fear and loathe, that his slave has heard his message and is ready to obey him. As I have lived a mistress, believing myself born free, so I will live a slave, knowing that I was born in bondage. The difference is terrible, but as mistress I upheld the institution as ordained of God. As slave I shall at least have a fair opportunity to learn whether it was or not. But oh!" she continued in a milder tone, and her tears burst forth afresh, " why did he cradle me with his own pure offspring ? Why make of me his child, and teach me to call him ' father,' and thee, my mistress Ada, by the name of ' sister.' Why educate me for a condition in which the misery is proportionate to the mind, and which bestial ignorance alone makes endurable ? Has he refined and cultivated my sensibilities only that my torture may be the more exquisite ? But I will not complain. What right has a slave to complain, when no lash blisters her back and her blood cries not yet from the ground for vengeance ? And what right even then has he to cry, save in secret to God ? Tell him I am ready to be led forth in his rudest garments to his vilest work, to be worked as a slave, lashed as a slave—sold as a slave !

"But before I fall to that despised contempt in which no request of mine will be heeded, tell him that as a last and only favor, after which the lips of the slave shall be forever mute, I would that, for the love my mother bore him, he will take this little cross, and without changing its form, will have the lower part made to ensheath a dagger. These cross pieces upon which the arms of the Saviour were nailed shall be the hilt. And if, with it sheathed, I would lose my heaven, with it unsheathed, I shall save my heaven."

"Nay, my daughter, you mistake the object of my visit," said the priest. "I come not from your father ; nor can I convey to him your answer. But unhappily, he seeks not to employ your comeliness upon the labor of his plantation. The purchaser in whose arms he would find a market for you is the pretended college student, the smooth-cheeked Defoe. I saw him in your company to-night ; and though I saw him but imperfectly, and so disguised as to make him appear much younger than he really is, his voice and form I knew—they were unmistakable ; and even had I not learned of his presence here, and come in pursuance of it, I should have recognized him. Accomplished, skillful, and of wonderful powers of deception and fascination, he is nominally the lieutenant, but really the ruling spirit of Lafitte. His career is written in blood and tears. Hell holds no scoundrel of a blacker die."

"Reverend father, though thou seemst, I believe such tales are false," exclaimed Julia, in a voice of smothered indignation.

"Would for thy sake," said the friar, calmly, "that what I say were false! But visit not upon the revealer of your fate the anger due to the authors of it."

"No, no," said Julia, tearfully, "forgive me, holy father; I know not what I say. But where have you learned of these horrors?"

"By your father's letter," replied the priest, handing it to her, "which was handed by the negro, Sandy, to your mother, on its way to Defoe; for it is through that faithful servant that she has been enabled thus far to watch over your welfare."

"My *master's* letter! Yes, it is in his hand—the same in which he has written me so many epistles full of kindly affection. Read it for me, good father; I cannot." And sinking upon a couch, and burying her face in her hands, she wept violently.

The priest read:

" LINDENHALL,

" My Dear Defoe :—

" I was grieved to learn by the propositions
contained in your last letter, that the only terms upon
which you will furnish me with the funds necessary
to save my family from ruin and myself from bank-
ruptcy, are the surrender to you of a person who,
though legally my slave, is in fact my child. You
will acknowledge the sacrifice I am making to you ;
for could I wait but a few years, her intelligence and
beauty, united as they are with the most amiable disposition, could not fail to secure for me through her
an alliance, by marriage, with some of the 'first families' of the South—a connexion which would ensure
me treble what I can get for her as a slave, even from
you. Such was my design in rearing and educating
her. But I can fully sympathize with the companion
of my boyhood in the intensity of his wishes in such
a matter, and I trust you will believe that my old
friendship for you is my strongest inducement for
taking this step. After all, however, the girl Julia is
but a chattel ; and though I thought of passing her
off as my child and as white, my duty to myself and
my creditors in my present embarrassments, makes
such benevolence too expensive a luxury. It would
be nothing more or less than a cheat to deceive the
world as to her rightful condition ; and the best course

is to let her occupy the position for which nature and her birth designed her.

"One thing, however, I require, my dear chum, or the matter might create a stir. Nothing must be done by force. Her consent must be obtained, so that she can never charge me with her misfortune. But you know what every woman is at heart, and these quadroons are naturally of easy affections. The task will not be a difficult one. Make yourself spruce and young. Look just as when I last saw you ten years ago, and you will do. She is pious as an angel, and you had better assume some suitable character. A show of money would have no effect whatever, as she is too foolish to be attracted by it. Play a cautious game until the bird is in the cage, for she knows more than both of us. Above all, come quickly, as I want the money and you the game. Hoping to welcome you soon to Lindenhall to a skillful siege, and easy conquest, and a rich booty,

"I remain your tried friend,

"BUTLER PRESTON."

"Holy Father!" exclaimed Julia as the letter closed. "No! no! still I cannot believe it. My father may be a fiend: I never loved him, but my Walter—gentle Walter, with whom in our infancy I have prayed by the bedside of his dying mother—he

a seducer, he a pirate and a fiend !   Sooner will I believe the sun sheds darkness, or that angels sin.   Oh,
father, though it caused the heavens to fall to the
earth, and shiver the world from its foundations, if I
were asked for my heart's love I could but answer,
' My dear Walter has it.'   For he came to me as no
wicked man could come, and all that was true and
good in my nature was so attracted by his greater truth
and goodness, that I could but yield to his power, as
a lesser planet revolves around a greater.   My whole
soul was drawn to him, I yearned for him, and my
powerless arms could not withhold, but stretching out
fondly enfolded him, and my lips were thrilled with
his kiss of plighted love as the trembling harps of heaven thrill at angels' touch.   Holy father," she cried,
rising, " I will rush to him, I will tell him all, and all
shall be explained."

" Hold !" said the priest, firmly and authoritatively
laying his hand upon her arm, " such rashness would
only be my death.   Did he know of my presence here
I should die.   But, come, he is now probably conversing with your father in the library : if there is a place
where you may listen I doubt not you may satisfy
yourself."

Almost overwhelmed by the weight of her grief, yet
not unwilling to embrace any opportunity of gaining
new light upon the matters revealed by the priest,

whose whole manner seemed indicative only of a kind and pure intent, and animated by the possible chance of explaining away that part of the story which pointed to the guilt of Defoe, she readily assented to this proposal, and Julia, followed by Ada and the priest, glided quickly and stealthily down the stairs and along the hall to a small closet or recess, entered by an adjoining room and opening into the library. Crouching down they listened to a few words, apparently the conclusion of a conversation between Preston and Defoe.

" So, captain, it is fully understood that you are to pay me five thousand francs as soon as Julia shall be placed on board the Flying Scud, at New Orleans ?"

Was it some superhuman power that pressed down the shriek that trembled upon Julia's lips as she heard, in the calm voice of him in whom her soul had trusted, the answer—

" Yes."

" And the balance of the thirty thousand when she shall have been safely conveyed to Barrataria, precisely as agreed in your letter." continued the stony voice of Preston.

" Exactly."

." You already boast of being certain that she will consent ?"

" I know that she suspects not the slightest deception, and were I really the chicken she mistakes me for, she could not love me more."

"You will proceed to-morrow, then, for New Orleans, to make the necessary arrangements for caging the bird and the payment of the first instalment."

"If you will furnish me with a horse and guide I will proceed to-night. If, as you think, her mother has got wind of the matter, delay is dangerous, and we must act promptly and immediately, 'peaceably if we can, but forcibly if we must.'"

"Well said, old chum. 'Faint heart never won fair lady.' But d— my soul if I ever saw a scoundrel who had passed through quite as much blood and thunder as you, come out at your age with such a devilishly innocent and sanctified appearance. I couldn't have believed it. Why, d— me, you are just the man for the part. No wonder the wench works well. I'll back you, captain, against the world."

"That you may, friend Preston," replied Defoe with a laugh, "but ring for the horse and nigger, and I will slope immediately."

"That's the talk. I think Sandy is waiting, for I hear a noise as if some one was up in the house."

Julia sunk insensible to the floor, and, as quietly as possible, the priest and Ada removed her to her room.

Within an hour a party of two on horseback, Defoe, and his guide Sandy, whose acquaintance we have made in a former chapter, set out by one direction from Lindenhall. They parted from Mr. Preston at the front door of the hall with a cordial grasp of the hand of Defoe, and a wish for his success.

Scarcely had the sound of their horses' hoofs ceased to be heard among the rustling leaves of the wood, before another party of two, the priest and Julia, closely mantled, entered a small row-boat that lay in a concealed nook of the river, underneath the dark shadows of a cluster of cypress that stood in a retired part of the ground.

The overwhelmed and almost insane Ada accompanied them to the shore, begged earnestly and even piteously to be permitted to accompany them, but was by both as earnestly persuaded to remain. With warm embraces and many tears, and a heartfelt prayer of each that heaven might save the other from every danger and be with them both forever, the sisters sadly parted, and Ada, standing upon the shore, watched and wept till the little skiff was lost in the mist of night, and then returned to the hall and to her couch, but not to repose.

CHAPTER VI.

THE COUNCIL.

" If we should wait till you in solemn council
With due deliberation had selected
The smallest out of four-and-twenty evils,
I' faith we should wait long.
Dash and through with it—that's the better watchword,
Then after, come what may come."   Piccolomini.

Upon the wings of the wind, or which is much the same, of the imagination, let us away to one of the wharves of New Orleans. Gazing around at the numerous and varied craft which line the levee, our attention is arrested by one whose sailing qualities would strike a sailor, as certainly as her beauty of build would please the least experienced eye, or her particular business puzzle a Custom-house officer.

A little three-cornered pennant drooping from the mast-head of the cutter announces her as the "Flying Scud." The Scud is a sharp, narrow, schooner-rigged vessel, of hardly sixty tons, with raking masts and clipper built, resembling our modern yachts in her length of beam and sprea of canvass. Three or four

stout, sinewy sailors, evidently full of nerve and mus-
cle, and bronzed under the suns and storms of so many
climes that they have lost all nationality of appearance, lounge carelessly around the forecastle, or with
a sailor's love of liberty, look listlessly over the levee,
and down into the town, as if there are those there
whose jovial rollicking they contemplate with envy.

Ever and anon they glance with the same careless,
listless hopefulness at the entrance to the cabin, as if
expecting its doors to open and with it their release ;
but they do not open.

Behind those doors and within that little cabin,
bent earnestly forward until their faces almost meet
over the narrow table between them, sit two persons,
in whose widely contrasted lineaments and appearance,
it seems difficult to discern the affinity which brings
them thus even though temporarily together.

The first is a young man, who may be thirty, or
even more, but who, at the first glance, might be
readily mistaken for one not older than twenty-two.
His high, intellectual forehead, regular and handsome
features, and dark, long and flowing hair, falling even
to his shoulders, are heightened in their effect by the
raven beard which sweeps his breast. His small and
delicate hand, with soft tapering fingers, a lady might
envy, while his graceful and manly form seems, at first
sight, inspired in its erect carriage by a manly mind:

He smiles. What can be more pleasant or winning than that smile ? No trace of impurity or guile seems to dwell in its open simplicity. What a delicate curling of the lips—how placid the brows as a moon-lit lake at evening—how soft and pleasant the expression of the eye ! And, too, that frank and open language of the whole countenance, would rob the shrewdest detective of his faintest suspicion.

But look ! the tenor of his thoughts has changed, and with it, the smooth brows are contracted into a mad frown ; the pleasant lip wreathes a smile of proud scorn, and the dark, handsome eye flashes a scowl of hatred ! and the delicate feminine hand is clenched fiercely above his head, and then brought down upon the table with a force which startles his companion from his revery, and makes every fragile article in the cabin ring under the blow.

Young man, we need see no more to prove how the thunder cloud and the rainbow lower and smile together in your character. Dark passions now speak from his bold countenance, and the precipitation of an angel from the realms of purity and bliss to the nether depths of misery, never wrought greater contrast than the apparent change by which his smile thus ends in a scowl.

A wide contrast exists between him and his companion. The latter a short, stout, thickset man, powerfully athletic in appearance, exhibites in his broad, weatherbeaten, ill-favored countenance and passionate eye, little evidence that the kindlier feelings ever reign where the ruder if not the brutal qualities undoubtedly predominate. His short, thick neck gives him a squat appearance, which a slight squint of his left eye either partially caused or concealed, or both, by a habit of closing that eye, and leaning his head over to the right, as if his neck had been designed expressly for the halter, does not by any means relieve.

Added to this, his face is thickly freckled and overhung by hair, originally of a red, fiery hue, enough to enrage the heart of a Spanish bull, but which fifty winters have streaked with frightful grizzly locks of white. A low, vulgar cunning, which could scarcely be dignified by the term intellect, glistens in his eye, and his whole appearance is fierce and vulgar. In keeping with this is his dress, which consists of a much soiled red flannel jerkin covering a shirt of the same material, and a pair of closely fitting blue trowsers, bound at the waist by a belt, from behind which the blade of a bowie-knife appears. A moment's closer observation, however, would reveal to the observer that there is one quality which might form the leading, perhaps the sole chord of affinity between two

such spirits. An expression of devil-may-care reck-
lessness predominates in the faces of both.

"I tell you, Conrad," said the elder of the two,
"to nab the wench at home. It's your only go, and
that now. These parts are getting hot as hell, and
we must change berths soon. Time's life to us."

"I see no danger, captain, as long as Preston is
true," replied the person addressed as Conrad.

"D—— Preston. He's a villain, it's true—double
dyed, but howsomdever I can't trust him. These vil-
lains that's not brought up to the trade like us, but
kinder take to it nat'rally—the devil can't trust. I
hate him. Why don't he come out and be one of
us ?"

"He's of more service to us where he is, Lafitte,"
suggested Conrad.

"We are of more service to him," returned the
captain, "or at least have been till lately, and now
that we are not likely to be of much more, that's just
the reason why I am afraid he'll peach."

"He'll not be likely to let out much after we've
got this girl," remarked Conrad.

"No," replied the pirate, "or we shall let her out,"
instinctively clutching and drawing partially from the
scabbard the bowie knife which hung at his side.
"Again, I say," growled the pirate, "the only way
to accomplish this piece of crack-brained nonsense of

yours is to start at dusk to-night, with a picked crew, for Preston's. You will reach there and lynch the girl by twelve, and, sunrise will see us with your lady in the cabin of the swiftest sail in port, with thirty guns and fifty men to guard her, and *ourselves* ten miles below New Orleans."

"Good !" said the youth, enthusiastically. "Win her first, and court her afterwards at leisure—that's according to the tactics of our craft."

"Bravo ! what could be better? Go there, place yourself a whole month in the power of Preston—and all for what ?—to get a girl's consent when you could just as well have her without. Catch me or you in that trap—not while my name's Lafitte. D—— me !"

"But, then," mused Conrad, more to himself than to his listener, "I have heard much of this lady, and I have a sort of presentiment that I shall love her, not as a pirate, but as a husband, and that she will somehow or other be a sort of star in my pathway—a sort of destiny to lead me on."

"Humph !" said Lafitte—"depends altogether on how you train her. I've known the puniest, shilly-shalliest women, when they've took a fancy to a man like us, after being deceived and a little abused, so as to find out what we are at last, throw away their prayer-books, and go into life with us with ten times more of the devil in them than the best of us. Women are strange things. The Lord knows that, as they are brought up ashore, tender as birdlings, and feeble as flowers, and silly as lambs, they are not made for the likes of us. But somehow or other there isn't the man, that is half a man, that can't get the love of any woman of his rank in life, if he works for it; and when that's done, no matter how they deal with others, they all act alike to the man they love. Women are either angels or devils. The devils are best for our mode of life. Train her into a devil, boy; it won't take long, if she's a girl of spirit."

"But is there no danger that we shall needlessly offend Preston, by thus throwing aside his offer, and taking the matter into our own hands? Though not worth much as a friend, he would be powerful as a foe. Besides, after all, she is his daughter, and as such he has always regarded her; and his feelings as a father might prompt him to something rash, if wounded."

"Ha! ha! Preston's feelings as a father! ha! ha!" laughed the pirate, with a bitter, ironical sneer, as if there was something in the falsehood which the words expressed which even he could look down upon and despise. "I warrant you against all harm from that quarter. I never knew a slaver yet that wouldn't sell every child that the law gave him a right to. He has sold her already, and I warrant you against all conscientious scruples on his part as to the manner of her delivery."

   ❂   ❂   ❂   ❂   ❂   ❂   ❂   ❂

As the dusky shades of twilight fell upon the city, and the dull lamps came, one by one, glimmering forth in its streets, a yawl, manned by six stout mariners, launched from the stern of the " Scud," and came around to her side. Here and there beneath their clothing one might have detected the outline of a pistol or the handle of a bowie. They were armed to the teeth, and evidently bound upon such a mission as the covert of the stealthy moon, rather than the open light of day would most favor. Arrived at the vessel's side, Lafitte, leaving the young and ardent Conrad, with whom he had been conversing, stepped down into the yawl, and in another moment they were out into the stream and pulling steadily up its current.

CHAPTER VII.

THE BROTHERS.

"His heart was formed for softness—warped to wrong,
Betrayed too early and beguiled too long,
Each feeling pure as falls the dripping dew
Within the grot, like that had hardened too ;
Less clear perchance, its earthly trial passed,
But sunk and chilled and petrified at last."—BYRON.

THE half-moon, which now and then stole fitfully forth from its covert among the clouds of the zenith at the departure of Lafitte and his confederates, had now nearly sunk behind the thicker night clouds of the west.   The city was shrouded in silence, except where, in some low saloon or place of carousal and debauch, the drunken ditty and obscene jest brought forth peals of sad laughter to mock the holy influence of the night's stillness.   The quays and resorts of business were deserted, and naught moved along the forests of masts which lined the levee except the soft measured plashing of the rippling waves, as they struck the sides of the vessels.   But still Conrad lingered upon the deck of the "Scud," now leaning over the vessel's side and looking down into the water, as if striving to read in its smooth surface the unknown story of the future—now gazing up among the flying, fitful clouds, and now sitting long and thoughtfully upon a low stool, with his arm dangling over the gunwale of the cutter. His air of deep abstraction was such as we have seen some young men wear, when it seemed as though they had arrived at a turning point, a fork in the roads of life, and were in doubt for a long and painful period which to pursue. Perhaps it might have been so with him, perhaps not, but whatever may have been the occasion or theme of his meditations, the silent passage of midnight did not interrupt the tenor of his revery. The doors of the cabin opened, and a dark-eyed and beautiful girl, of hardly more than twenty years, stole softly to his side and laid her hand a moment upon his shoulder. But the hand was scarcely noticed, and its owner, as if taking this for an intimation that her presence was at that moment unwelcome, as silently retired. Probably his revery might have continued until the city bells, now tolling the requiem of the dying day, chimed in merry welcome of the rising sun, had it not been gently broken by the low, servile inquiry coming from a dark skin and bowing form, whose voice is familiar to us—

" Am dis Massa Conrad ?"

The skipper turned to the quay, and in a moment

recognizing the voice and form together, exclaimed—
" Why, Sandy, what the devil brings you here !
Any word from your master ?"

" Not 'zackly," said Sandy, revealing two long rows
of nature's dentistry with an apparent delight, which
in a person of any other race it would have been difficult to account for, but which, in a negro, is merely
the natural consequence of having been spoken to by
a white man.

" Well, what's up ?"

" I dunno, massa," said the negro, still grinning and
working his body into an amiable squirm, as if trying
to think what he came for.

" Well, what do you want ?"

" Dunno, massa," replied Sandy, in whose countenance the distortions were by this time growing
frightful.

" Well, what the devil are you here for ?"

" Dunno, massa," reiterated the negro after a slight
pause, from whom every vestige of his mission seemed
entirely to have disappeared.

" Who sent you, you blackskin ?" said the skipper
angrily.

' I wish I knew, massa—but I dunno, Sandy so fus-
ticated ; heah ! He dunno nuffin, nor that either.
He allers did know that ar much till he cum here.   I
beg pardon, massa, I go back and ax him," said the

slave, his eyes brightening at this happy method of extricating himself from his quandary.

Conrad eyed the poor fellow for a moment, as if doubtful whether to laugh at the ridiculous absurdity of his position, or, after the most approved custom, to break his skull for him.

"Did he send you a letter or anything for me ?" he demanded at length.

"Ho ! be sure he did, massa ;" said Sandy suddenly, at the same time diving energetically into one after another of the recesses of his wardrobe, and finally producing, to his infinite gratification, the billet whose delivery constituted the object of his mission—"be sure ; why how forgitful nigger's is—ain't dey, Massa Conrad ?   I'm so glad I thought of it at last, he ! he !" and Alexander grinned with as much complacency, and far more genuine enjoyment, than that with which his great namesake swayed the sceptre over a world subdued.

The skipper took the letter, and directing Sandy to wait, retired a moment into the cabin. An exhausted wick was burning in the socket upon the table, and by that he first rapidly, then measuredly and half in mystery perused the letter. In a moment he returned to the deck, and first examining carefully a brace of richly wrought and engraved pistols, and having satisfied himself that they were properly loaded and primed, and giving a rap on the scuttle which brought up two drowsy tars to watch on deck, he directed the slave carelessly to lead the way.

They stepped upon the levee together, and went down through the muddy, dingy, glimmering streets of the city. After a short walk, Sandy stopped before a medium looking frame house, over the low door of which was displayed the sign " Hotel d' Espagnol," into which they entered, and, passing through the bar-room, the skipper, with an air half jaunty, half watch-ful, suffered himself to be led into a small, retired room, in the middle of which was a single table, with two chairs by it, in the opposite one of which a person was sitting.

As the waiter retired, and the door closed upon them, the two persons gazed at each other for a moment, and then the last comer, with a calm, indifferent air, took the vacant seat, and looked across it at his companion in silence. No word or sign of greeting passed between them.

Their features were strangely alike. Scarcely could a resemblance have been more marked and perfect. It was almost a reflection. Save that a few scarcely per-ceptible wrinkles gathered around the eye of the last comer, and here and there a thread of gray strayed from his crown in disagreeable contrast with the re-mainder of his jet black locks, and perhaps, as we now see him, save also the gathering scowl of ill passions which seem to speak forth from his once over handsome face like the lightning flash from the thunder cloud, and which contrast forcibly with the calm, earnest, and thoughtful expression of the other's countenance, over which, perhaps, a few less winters may have passed, and a few less vicissitudes—with these exceptions, the likeness seems, as we have said, more like a reflection than a resemblance. The skipper was the first to break the silence.

"My brother, I suppose," he said calmly, his voice firm, and not abating in its sternness.

"Yes," spoke the other.

A pause succeeded, in which the eye of the elder person wandered occasionally, and restlessly, from the other to various objects around, none of which, however, he seemed to see, while the other looked at him with a steady and serious eye, unaverted.

"She—is *she*—living?" resumed Conrad at length, though at this question his voice trembled, and he feigned to brush his handsome hair back from his forehead and temples, that he might, unobserved, wipe a tear from his eye.

"Our mother is dead—long ago. She died in my childhood," replied the other, whom the reader has already recognized as Walter Defoe.

Conrad breathed a sigh, as if relieved, and continued—

" She never knew of my life after I left home ?"

"I think," said Walter, " I think, my brother, that she knows of it now—has always looked down upon you, and watched over your every step. Brother, have you never heard her whisper, or felt her presence ?"

Conrad bit his lip in anger, and for a moment a pallor overspread his countenance ; but it instantly vanished, and was replaced by a cool smile of skeptical assumption and self-complacency.

" No, Walter," he said calmly, " I have neither seen nor heard her. If I had, I might have been a different man. And such has been my life, that this very fact proves to me that she neither hears nor sees aught of me, for if there is such a thing as a spirit I know she would have appeared and spoken to me. I wish these religious vagaries were true. But I have studied them to the bottom ; they are false. Religion is a farce—piety a delusion—heaven a scheme—hell a scarecrow—and God an invention of the human imagination. Thank God—if I may say so, when I believe in no such thing as a God—I have one comfort which sustains me in my mode of life, and leaves me free to enjoy myself ! I am an infidel. My God is myself ; my heaven and my hell are here ; and the grave is a finality. Take away these truths, and I am a wretch."

"And with them, you are a—*pirate!*" pursued Walter, calmly.

He had well nigh suffered for his temerity ; for scarcely had the last word fallen from his lips, ere Conrad, with a bound, stood over him, with his fingers clutched in a choking grasp upon his neck-band, and Walter saw the point of the bowie knife glistening at his breast. His face livid with rage, and his eyes glaring like a demon's, the pirate stood a moment thus, glanced hesitatingly around, and then, as if controlled by a second thought, quietly releasing his hold, resumed his seat, saying, in the same calm voice, as if nothing had occurred—

"How do you know that ?"

"From Mr. Butler Preston ?"

"Preston !"

"The same. And my business with him has brought me to you. I will tell you all, for I desire your concert and action, or at least your forbearance, in a matter upon which my life and happiness depend. I met his daughter, Miss Preston——"

"Which one ?"

"Miss Julia Preston ; first at the couch of our sick mother, whom she used often to visit, with a kindness worthy of an angel, and afterwards at a northern boarding-school."

" Yes, you loved her.   Well !"

" From what I saw of her there, I was induced to hope that our acquaintance might ripen into intimacy, and for that purpose I left college, after a few months, as she had unfortunately returned to her home, and came on-to New Orleans."

" Well—you saw her ?"

" After some search, I at last found her whereabouts ; and on arriving at the residence of her father, a few miles from here, great was my surprise to find myself welcomed to the hospitality of his house and the society of his daughters, as an old acquaintance of his, though I had never seen or heard of him prior to my arrival at New Orleans."

" The d——l it was !"

" Still greater was my surprise when I learned that this welcome arose from the supposition by Mr. Preston that I was yourself, whom I supposed to be dead, but whom he seems to have well known some twelve or fifteen years ago."

" And so you played the part of Conrad Defoe with the old fool !"

" The part was in a manner thrust upon me ; and ascertaining that it would answer my laudable purpose for the time, and moreover, that it was somehow involved with facts which it was important for me, as an honorable suitor for the lady's hand, to know, I did continue to wear the assumed character."

" You won her love ?" snarled Conrad, impatiently.

" I believe so."

" You believe so ! Yes ; so do I. What then brings you to me ?"

" The fact that this young lady—though pure and lofty as the stars of heaven ; a high-souled Christian ; an accomplished and lovely woman, gifted with all that could unite to make woman attractive—is not a free agent, but a chattel, entitled by law only to yield to the will of creatures as far beneath her as earth is beneath heaven. The fact that she has been sold, and is soon to be delivered, body and soul, to you, to be at best a soulless plaything in your hands, or who knows but ultimately a shameless outcast among outlaws ?   Will you bring this doom upon one whom you have but casually seen, and whom you can neither love nor hate ? Oh, spare her ! Spare for the sake of the dear and virtuous mother who kissed you in your infancy ! Spare, oh, spare her," cried Walter, kneeling before his brother, who hid his bowed face in his hands, and taking his brother's hand in his— " for the sake of the chaste maiden you once loved, and whom God removed from your very arms for the company of heaven ; Spare her for the sake of the innocence of your own infancy, to which, would to God you might return !   Spare her, O my brother, for the sake of him who still loves you with a brother's love, and who now and always yearns for you to leave your wandering life of evil and of misery, and come and find a home with him !   Spare her for the sake of her own pure soul, which living, will pray for and bless you, and having arisen to heaven, will intercede before the throne of that God who does exist, for your forgiveness !   For your brother's sake ; for your mother's sake ; for heaven's sake, and for the lovely Julia's sake, spare her from such a fearful and horrible doom ! Why if you will not, but will insist upon carrying out this nefarious and diabolical scheme, you cannot make her outlive wrongs at which devils would hide their faces and weep.   The very earth shall yawn beneath, and a dagger, wafted up by the pity of the bottomless pit, shall be placed in her hand.   When you have won her, you will have won a corpse.   O brother ! the heart of your mother is speaking in those tears. Will you not spare her ?   Speak—I know you have done so already in your heart.   Let not an opportunity of redeeming the worst act of your lifetime elude your grasp.   It is before you now.   Seize it !"

"I do !" said Conrad, weeping audibly.

"She is yours forever."

"Heaven bless you," replied Walter.

"But hold," said Conrad. "Determining not to trust to the precise terms which Preston offered me, I have this night sent a detachment of men to seize her, and she is ere this in their custody."

"Holy heaven, forbid it!" Walter ejaculated.

"It is too late now to forbid or to prevent it. Before daylight they will have conveyed her apast the city down to the bend, where she will, unless prevented, be embarked upon the 'Scud,' and a few days will land her at Barrataria."

"How can this be prevented?" groaned Walter.

"In this way. You, with a dozen picked men from the Scud, and I with another crew, will watch the river and stop Lafitte with the yawl as they pass.— Miss Preston shall be rescued, and the next packet for New-York shall convey you safely to your homes."

They rose, and leaving the Hotel d'Espagnol, in a few minutes Walter found himself in the stern of a small open boat upon the opposite side of the river, and temporarily in command of as rough looking a crew of cut-throats as ever boarded an East Indiaman or made an unfortunate prisoner walk the death plank.

CHAPTER VIII.

THE BITER BIT.

"I will discover such a horrid treason,
As, when you hear 't, and understand how long
You've been abused will run you mad with fury."
       BEAUMONT and FLETCHER.

GREAT was the surprise of Mr. Preston, when, on returning from his ride over the plantation on the morning following the departure of Defoe and Sandy, he learned that Julia also was missing, and, after a thorough search, could not be found. We cannot say that he was grieved, though he may naturally have recoiled from a contemplation of the effect which a discovery of his schemes, when made by Julia, must have had upon the pure heart of one who had been to him so fond and apparently loving a child. But it placed him in a quandary of doubt, in which the more he endeavored to see his way clearly, the denser grew the fog.

Two suppositions only occurred to him. One was that Julia had in some way discovered his intentions and fled to avoid their fulfillment. But in what way? Defoe himself could not certainly have informed her.

It would but frustrate a scheme which that person had as much at heart as himself. But no other person had access to her who was at all acquainted with it. At first it occurred to him that Ada might possess some clue to the mystery. But her frantic grief and distracted manner ever since Julia's flight was known to the household, made it painful for him to address her, and moreover convinced him that she could not be a party to it, and besides he had not sufficient confidence in her strength of mind to believe that she could act a dissembled part or retain so long anything which was really a secret.

This supposition vanished from his mind, therefore, almost as readily as it had occurred. The only one remaining was, that of Defoe had foreclosed the agreement between them in a summary manner, by inducing Julia to fly with him. Defoe's arch subtlety he had never doubted, and during his late stay at Lindenhall, it had sometimes been exerted so skillfully that Preston himself often felt half deceived by it, and could scarcely believe his guest was the veritable Conrad Defoe of his youthful days, and whose name carried terror through the Gulf, second only to that of Lafitte.

People who are controlled by but one strong motive, easily transfer that motive upon others in passing judgment upon their acts. Preston could conceive of

no other motive than cupidity, which would have in-
fluenced him to act in like manner under the same
circumstances, and it is not strange that he who was
so treacherous to others, easily came to the conclusion
that he was the pitiable victim of a scheme by which
he had been swindled out of his child, or what was in
his eyes more valuable, his chattel; and, as he now
began to think, his dearest and warmest feelings had
been grossly outraged and wounded by a renegade,
who would leave him to whistle for the heavy sum
which he had sacrificed so much to ensure, and which
was necessary to preserve his standing in society, not
only as a man of family and wealth, but as a man of
honor.   Not long did he calmly revolve this theory in
his mind.   Stung to the quick at the bare apprehension of such an injury, he instantly set about the
means to defeat it, or if that was impossible, to avenge
it.   The latter task he thought could be managed in
a way as harmless to himself as it would be certain in
its results.   In a moment he too had mounted the
best horse upon the plantation, and leaving the latter
in the care of a venerable old negro, he without guide
or companion set out at a rapid pace for the city.   As
he rode through the quarters, not an eye met his of the
many ignorant, degraded, almost heathen Africans who
performed the labor of his plantation, but was dimmed
with tears which would not dry, at the loss of their

angel mistress. Poor creatures! Brutal and selfish and half savage as they were, it is doubtful whether there was one among them who would not cheerfully have given up his own life to have saved from injury one whom all loved so much. The faith of the pious was shaken at the thought that harm could follow so good and pure a creature.

"Deah me!" said old aunt Tanzey, as she shaded her eyes with her hand, and from the door of her rude cabin of logs and mud watched the receding form of the proud planter—"deah me! if harm do come to angel like Miss July, who *will* de Lord help?"

"Nebba feah—nebba feah," said her good old man uncle Tim, holding up his hands devoutly—"De Lord will take care ob missus. He got her now in de holler ob he hand, or old Tim no prophet. Mind when you heah from her, you heah dat dis day—dis how she safe—tank de Lord. Else dares no vartue in ole Tim. Didn't ole Tim look ober his right shoulder at de new moon last night, and did you eber know anyting bad to happen arter he'd done that? All's well. Mind old Tim. Mind him."

Ah! how upon the book of the recording angel compared the simple, honest feelings of those poor chattels, with the talented and accomplished villainy of their lordly proprietor; contrasting the sphere given them and the manner in which they had filled it, theirs

would have been like an inscription in gold upon a
ground of black ; his like stains of black upon a
ground of gold.

The sun was approaching the horizon when he arrived in the city. A short ride brought him upon its
principal street, upon which were the offices of the
Governor and Mayor of the city. The latter and then
the former he entered, where his appearance or mission
seemed to create an unusual stir. In less than half
an hour a strong, fully equipped and armed body of
some two hundred men rapidly passed under a quiet
review, at the rooms of a hotel near the City Hall.
There they remained until past twelve o'clock at night,
when, at a signal, they issued forth in citizens' dress,
and in small, irregular squads, and proceeding to the
levee, in a short time swarmed out upon the river.

CHAPTER IX.

EVIL COMPANY.

"Friend to the sea, and foeman sworn
To all that on her waves are borne."—ROKEBY.

IN a recent chapter we left young Walter Defoe in the midst of his novel associates, from whom, as he looked around upon them more deliberately, his first instinctive wish was to extricate himself, but a second thought told him they were the necessary means to accomplish a great purpose, upon which his life's happiness, and the life and honor of one dearer to him than life depended, and he submitted to his embarrassed position. From the singularity of his immediate position, his mind reverted to the chain of novel vicissitudes which seemed to have attended his whole adventure of love, and which, a short time before, would have seemed to him like the dream of a romancer, rather than a succession of actual events.

But the vicissitudes through which he had passed were not more strange than the issue now before him was exciting and important. The " Scud " had already dropped down the river, and rumors afloat through the town of a strong and well organized plot for the capture of some suspected vessel now in harbor, made their stay every moment more dangerous, and the facts that the Scud would never return to New Orleans, when her captain and crew were once more safe upon her decks, and consequently that Julia, if their expedition had been successful, would be borne away never to return, were to the mind of Walter both morally certain.

" Can it be," said he, " that within these few moments, upon this quiet river, and depending upon the fitful coming and going of these obscuring mists, through which I can scarcely see the lights on the levee, this greatest question of my life, and the great crisis of hers, hangs like a world upon nothing ? Is there no providence to overrule and govern these things ? Do issues so great as the life's happiness of one human soul, and the eternal welfare of another, depend upon causes so shadowy as the coming and going of these thin night mists ?" Amidst thoughts like these the awaiting lover had unconsciously fallen into a revery, and did not notice that one after another until three boats had almost simultaneously appeared in the river, either of which might have been, for aught he or the drowsy tars. at the oars observed, the one for which they were in wait and watching Just at this moment, not from either of those boats, but apparently from some one which had been skirting close under the shadow of the levee, came the loud, shrill shriek of a female—" help !"

But once the shriek was uttered, but that once was enough ; and the fact that it came not again added to its terrible power.   He thought he recognized it as the voice of Miss Preston.

" Spring to it, lads," cried Walter, and in another moment, under the quick, powerful strokes of their oars, they were bounding in the direction from which the shriek was heard.   Now it is in sight, and Walter discerns in the rear the form of a short, thick-set and powerful man, to whom his conceptions easily gave the name of Lafitte.   He held in his arms a burden, at the sight of which Walter trembled in every nerve, and over which another outlaw, equally powerful, suspended a drawn and glistening sabre.

" Thank God," thought Walter, " it will soon be over, and Julia will be saved."   The boats had nearly touched.   The oarsmen were about to rest upon their oars, when those in each simultaneously discovered, by the light of morning which was now dawning, in their stern and upon either side of them, and rapidly making for their front, though at some distance, a swarm of boats, swiftly rowed and heavily manned, while the loud report of a volley of rifles, and the noise of their

5

balls as they went swiftly by, left the pirate bands no longer unconscious of their danger. In a moment a return of their fire found its victims in every pursuing boat, and now, amidst the groans of the wounded and the shouts of the enraged pursuers, commenced a fierce and doubtful contest of death and speed. The pirate boats had by some thirty strokes the start, and every conceivable motive to exertion, giving additional power to their sinewy arms, their boats shot through the water with steady and almost superhuman speed. The piers of the city danced rapidly behind them, and they were upon the open river amidst the open country. Bend after bend was skillfully rounded by both, yet the contest remained equal. Stroke after stroke, minute after minute, left them still the same. The contest hung doubtfully as by a thread, for the pursuers were in discharge of a great duty. The enemy of mankind, and the terror of their commerce, sat in yonder boat, now hastening to the successful completion of one of his darkest tragedies. Upon each pull of the oar depended the security of the seas, and the lives of helpless widows and orphans. Almost overcome with terror and grief at his false and anomalous position, as well as at the utter apparent failure of all his hopes, oh ! how Walter now wished himself at the head of that pursuing force, cheering them on and—but here a ball from the pursuing party shattered his arm, and seemed to enter his very heart. A whirling sensation that he was wounded, a feeling that he was dying came over him. He sunk in the stern of the boat, and as he placed his hand to his side it slipped in the oozing gore. His vision and his consciousness grew dim together. He thought he was lifted over the side of the boat, and that he sunk slowly and peacefully under the water. A confusion of wild, strange, fantastic thoughts filled his brain, among which none were distinct save the image of his mother and of Julia, whose name he murmured last as the waters closed over him, and he remembered no more.

CHAPTER X.

MIDNIGHT MADE DARKER.

" She is won! we are gone, over bank, bush, and scaur,
' They'll have fleet steeds that follow !' quoth young Lochinvar."
                                                    MARMION.

WHEN the last ripple of the waves, upon which floated away from her vision the fugitive Julia and the good father, had disappeared, the weeping Ada remained for a long time overwhelmed with grief, and riveted to the spot.   Up to this time, Julia had been both a sister and a mother to her ; for, though but a year her senior, Julia's naturally powerful mind, warm heart, and superior accomplishments, had fitted her for the bright star of whatever society should feel the magic influence of her presence ; but especially had she won from Ada that affectionate, up-looking, half-worshiping confidence with which the good, but weak, ever follow the good and strong. As from an inexhaustible, ever-welling fountain, she had, from her infancy, drawn from Julia's lips rich draughts of instruction, of practical philosophy, and of liberal, generous thoughts.   Her mind had seemed to the less brilliant

Ada a curious magazine of all that was useful and pleasing, and her heart of all that was lovely and pure. Indeed, whenever the amiable Ada, in prayer or in moments of silent communion and thought, or at any other time, had felt as if she ought to thank God for something, her heart irresistibly responded to the call for gratitude when she thought of the sweet sister which heaven had given her. To think how different might have been her lot—nay, her whole mind, and heart, and self, but for the influence of Julia; how lonely would have been the hours of her infancy, and how ill-informed and wayward she would have grown up! For Ada was a pliable and gentle, though affectionate thing, and felt that she was one of those who are fashioned in the mould of circumstances.

From the dawn of her infancy; through all the sports of childhood; in her girlhood's studies, and during the tedious hours of boarding-school life, not less than amidst the lordly and aristocratic solitude of Lindenhall, Julia had been with her. In the morning walk—at their toilet—in their forenoon ride, or by the piano—over the novel or the poem—floating in a tiny skiff among the winding, shady inlets of the river, or culling flowers by its banks—sleeping or waking—laughing or weeping—Julia's fond embrace had enclosed her until now; and in that embrace her life had passed like a dream of sunshine.

And now by power, as of a hideous, formless, shape-
less monster, which she. could scarcely comprehend
in its character, farther than to feel that it was terri-
bly evil, Julia had been torn from her, and for the first
time in all her life she felt a miserable, a horrid sense
of loneliness—a feeling as if she hung suspended and
alone in a dark void, with nothing to lean upon—
nothing to love—came over her, and her soul turned
from the world and the future, and from life in upon
herself, and she longed to die.

"Oh," thought she, "that I could have lived just
such a life as I have lived until this morning, and then
have died ! But now all is dark," she cried—"dark,
dark. Poor sister Julia ! poor me !"

But after a time better thoughts prevailed, and she
kneeled down upon the dewy verdure, there where the
sigh of the old and young pines seemed to mingle with
her voice, and the willow waved its long, weeping ten-
drils in sympathy, and the dark cypress wore its deepest shade of mourning, and prayed. The evil before
her was so mysterious, so overwhelming—the remedy
for it so indefinite, and the blight of a great misfortune
seemed so inevitable, that she could only pray that
God would look in pity upon her loved sister, and
shield her from all evil and from every foe.

When she rose to return to the old home of her infancy, the night was draped in that dense fold of dark-

ness which precedes the dawn. How changed were her feelings towards the venerable old mansion, hitherto so pleasant, but which she now trembled to enter —and almost a revulsion came over her as she noiselessly lifted the latch, and crossed the threshold. But a second thought assured her that whatever its inmates might be, the old house was as sinless and good as ever, and so she glided up silently to her room, and threw herself exhausted and weeping upon her bed.

No refreshing slumber visited her eyes. Her mind, with feverish activity, was following her sister and the holy father upon their toilsome night journey. The conduct of her father came up before her with a clearness and vividness with which she had never before seen it. The winning exterior and the innocent manner of Defoe, whom she had, until a few hours since, thought to be the only person in the wide world quite worthy of the love of Julia, presented themselves to her in vivid contrast with his, as she now thought, fully proved baseness ; and she longed, for once, for the power of a knght-errant of olden time, that she might go forth and rid the world of such monsters of wickedness. And then she thought of Julia—a slave and a fugitive—a thing she had been accustomed to hear of as being hunted into swamps, and jungles, and morasses, amid crocodiles and wild beasts, until neither men nor dogs could follow them farther, and there left to linger out a few years in a wild, laborious, lonely life, living friendly companionship with starvation and serpents, and fearing only dogs and men. True, she knew that no such a fate was in reserve for her sister. If the *finer* feelings of humanity would not save her from such a doom, there were others, unfortunately, that would reserve her for a worse. She thought of her sister, pure, elevated, and refined, cast upon the will of others, without friends, without protection, without home, without money, without even the ownership of her own person or the legal right to remain pure, and compelled perchance to associate with the vile and dissolute, too abandoned to stand in awe of that superiority which they could not but see, or to befriend the helpless orphan whom destiny had given them the chance to spit and trample upon.

She thought of all these things as she tossed restlessly upon her couch, until the slow steps of morning came, and one by one the stars disappeared, and the darkness grew slowly gray ; and at last streaks of light tinged the long straight clouds, till they became lurid, and then the sun fairly arose, and the morning advanced, and it was after the usual hour to rise. Still her hands clasped her sleepless lids, and her brain was racked with torture.

By-and-bye the faithful old house servant came to the door and knocked, and said—

" Miss Julia—Miss Ada !"

" Come in, Betsey," said Ada.

Betsey came in, and folding her hands, exclaimed—

" Why, bless us, wot de matta, Miss Ada ? De Lor' bless us ! whar Miss July—war Miss July ?"

" She has gone," said Ada, weeping again bitterly. " She has gone away entirely, and we shall never see her again.   Don't ask me where ; I don't know where. She is lost—and dead—and buried—and worse."

The old wench, as she left the room, burst out in loud sobs of—

" Poor missus ! De Lord help her, poor missus ; and save her, poor missus ; and bless her, poor—poor— poor——"

By this time she had reached the kitchen, and soon there was not a dry eye in Lindenhall. All were weeping for " poor missus." How remarkable !—chattels weeping in sympathy for chattels.

Late in the morning, her father returned from his usual ride over the plantation, but Ada did not seek him ; she could not. She had always been afraid of him—had never had the hardihood to give him her confidence ; and now she could not help feeling that she could regard him no longer as a father. She saw, however, the utter absence of parental grief, with which he heard the news of Julia's disappearance. It seemed to involve him in doubt, and he thought, but not in

sorrow.   She heard him in the library, walking measuredly and steadily up and down, as was his wont
when devising new plans for the improvement of his
plantation.   This lasted during the forenoon, and at
noon he suddenly mounted his horse and rode rapidly
away, and Ada was left the sole white person within
a circuit of many miles.   Yet the hearts of those
around her, though beating beneath tawny skins, beat
faithfully and truly, and there was not one of them in
whose custody she would not have felt secure.

Hour after hour, minute after minute of the remainder of the livelong day, passed wearily and tediously
away.   Never did a week seem so long to her as that
day.   It seemed as if the sun never would reach the
horizon.   Anon, the sorrowful Ada would rise from
her couch, and go down into the parlor.   But the
piano and the guitar were silent ; the bird was mute ;
tears were in the eyes of all she met, and every familiar object served only to recall to her mind her lost
sister.   Neither refreshment nor occupation could she
avail herself of.   Her mind could not fix upon the
one, and her palate sickened at the other.   At last,
however, evening came, and Ada, yielding to the ad-
monitions of the faithful old " Betsey," returned to
her couch.

For a long time her weary brain still wandered
wildly over the strange realities of the past few days,

and their bitter consequences ; but after it had been dark many hours, and the domestics of the hall had retired, and the little life of that little world was again hushed into perfect silence and repose, her exhaustion partially triumphed over her miseries, and she sunk into a dreamy, drowsing slumber. In her slumber, Julia came to her and took her hand, and began to converse with her ; but when Ada would have replied, she awoke, and the vision vanished. After finding it was but a dream, the poor girl closed her lids, and wished that dream might come again. Then as she passed again into slumber, Defoe came to her, and reasoned with her so calmly and earnestly in favor of his innocence, that her confidence in him was restored, and she was about to extend her hand to him, when she awoke and found that he too had vanished. 'Twas but a dream, and she returned once more to her slumbers, and wished for that dream also again. And then she thought a number of strange looking persons, none of whom she knew, stood by her, and that after a moment one of them lifted her slowly up from the couch in which she lay, mantling her form in the covering under which she was sleeping, and bore her softly down stairs ; but this seemed so wild and strange, that this she knew was a dream, and so she thought she would not awake or shriek, but would see the issue of the vision, which came to her almost with the vividness of reality.   Her next sensation after crossing the threshold, was of being at the shore of the river, where she had parted from Julia and the priest.   By what means she had come from the house there, she knew not ; but there, holding her in his strong arms like a plaything, was the very same man who had lifted her from her couch.   She seemed to see his features as distinctly as in the open day ; and around were the forms which had stood in her chamber, and down at the water's edge ; and within a few feet of her was a row-boat, filled with people of the same wild, uncouth, and even fierce expression.   So much like reality did it now appear to her, that she tried to shriek, but felt the hand of the strong man upon her mouth, so that she could not ; and sick with terror, and feeling that she had awoke, she waited a moment for the dream to pass, but it did not.

In a twinkling, still held by the same iron grasp, she was in the boat, the crew also ; and under the swift strokes of their oars, they were rapidly shooting down the river.   Then the horrid consciousness flashed upon her soul.   It was not a dream, but all a living and terrible reality !

"Oh, God !" she groaned—"oh, oh, God !" and sunk, in a lethargy of despair, powerless in the arms of her supporter.   How long she might have remained thus, silent and unresisting, she knew not.   For a time, whether for moments or hours she knew not, she was borne along by the almost superhuman speed of the rowers, down the river, in darkness, solitude, and silence. The hand was removed from her mouth ; she could have shrieked, but she cared not to. She felt as if her destiny was taken out of her own control, and she recked not what should become of her. Besides, had she shrieked, no human ear was near ; no human hand could have aided her. At last, after being borne along for several hours in this manner, she saw close upon her right here and there a light, and soon another and another. The lights approached and increased in numbers, and then she saw dimly through the mist here and there a spar—a mast—a chimney top, and at last a man moving along the levee. Quietly and calmly for a moment, she summoned all her energies, and then, without warning or changing her position, sent up, with the utmost of her power, one loud, shrill shriek for "Help !" It was this shout which Walter had heard as narrated in the last chapter. In another moment her face was so tightly gagged that she could scarcely breathe, and pinioned hand and foot, she was thrown rudely in the bottom of the boat ; but she knew that her effort had been successful, for in a moment after she heard the sharp, clattering reports of a volley of musketry, and the blood of those who were bearing her away flowed down around her. She looked out, and close beside her was a boat manned like their own, and in the stern stood—Walter Defoe. Alas! she thought, my dream of him was as false as himself. Here he stands forth in his true character—a pirate and a fiend. There is no longer any room for doubt. Rising convulsively, as well as she could, she looked for a moment at the boat, as if fearing it might contain some other form which she could recognize ; and then falling back, Ada clasped her pinioned hands and murmured—

"No, no, Julia is not there. Thank God, I can still hope she is safe !"

The volley which had been fired into their boat was answered by running shots from their own, and Ada discovered from the fierce excitement of those around her that they were being hotly pursued. But by whom ? How grateful she felt already to those who she believed must triumph ! How she wished she could assist them, or rise and encourage them in the task—but she could not. Amidst the blood and strife and shots thickly flying above her, the fancy even crossed her mind that they were led on by some bold generous youth, who when he saw her would love her, as she had often seen detailed in romances, and she even then made up her mind that if such a one did present himself, though he were the very quintessence of ugliness, she would perfect the romance by giving him her hand. Strange thought for such a moment—during her whole life before, she had never yet so much as thought of love.

Rising with difficulty, once more she caught sight of her persuers, rapidly but ineffectually following them, alternately cheering, shouting and firing. But in her own boat and in that immediately in their wake, were strong, sinewy and experienced men, struggling as if their very lives hung, as they did, upon the contest. Just then, after a solitary shot from their pursuers, she saw Defoe sink wounded and bleeding into the water. She could not but pity the poor fellow with whom she had spent so many pleasant moments, who seemed capable at least of so much that was generous and good, and whose guilty nature and guiltless appearance were to her so incomprehensible—and this spectacle, and the red gore which was flowing fast around her, and in which she almost lay, filled her heart with sickness. A mazy film gathered over her vision, and she saw no more until she felt herself upon the deck of a large schooner-rigged craft, and knew that her pursuers had been distanced, and were now kept at bay by the guns of the schooner, and that she was fully in the power of as veritable a legion of cutthroats as ever hoisted the pennant of the skull and cross-bones at their mast-head—and who were now with sails unfurled and a fair wind rapidly and securely bearing out to sea. She was then led into a tiny but beautiful cabin, resembling rather the bower of some eastern princess than a room in the craft of a buccaneer, richly hung with tapesty of velvet, inwrought with gold and silver, which, however, the poor girl had little disposition or intellect remaining to admire. A pretty and amiable waiting-maid removed the unsuitable and gory night-covering in which she was enveloped, and arrayed her form, now passive under despair, in a toilet very much after her own taste and fancy.

CHAPTER XI.

ADA AT SEA.

" Two things break the monotony
  Of an Atlantic trip,
Sometimes, forsooth, we ship a sea,
  Sometimes we see a ship."—Hood.

"————————I have dreamt thou wert
A captive in thy hopelessness; afar
From the sweet home of thy young infancy,
Whose image unto thee is as a dream
Of fire and slaughter: I can see thee wasting
Sick for thy native air."   L. E. L.

For several days scarcely an incident occurred to break the monotony of Ada's life on ship-board. Except the pretty and chatting waiting-maid Annette, who was constantly in attendance upon her, endeavoring, by every means in her power to please her, she saw no one.

At first the intense and agonizing excitement under which she had labored, rendered this monotonous quiet an agreeable relief, and she almost felt like thanking her malefactors for the interval they had left her for reflection. The " one fell swoop" which had stripped her of her home, and placed her powerless, in the midst of the most abandoned of men, was so unreal in its appearance, and so overwhelming that it blinded and confused her mental vision, and she could scarcely comprehend it, but moved, and spoke, and saw it all, as in a dream.

Sometimes she would be strangely calm, and her despair having seemed to conquer all her natural instincts, she would look forward to her new sphere of life, as if she were the submissive toy of destiny, ready to fill the sphere allotted to her, and to take upon her, without a pang, whatever form or character chance and circumstances might require. At others her very blood would boil at the outrage under which she suffered, and her gentle girlish soul, stung to madness by the thought of the dark prospect before her, would rave against mankind and curse her male-factors. In these moods the vision of death came to her like a pleasant thought, and she would resolve to put an end to an existence which had so little to hope and so much to fear. But to elude her misfortunes by this means was as impossible as by any other. She soon perceived that the shrewd Annette acted in the triple capacity of a faithful nurse, an amusing companion, and a watchful body-guard.

Not the slightest article by which she could, in these disordered moods, have put an end to her existence, was suffered to remain within her reach, and the ever-watchful Annette was every moment by her side, striving with the most amiable perseverance and tact, to relieve the tedium of the long hours and reconcile Ada to her new position.

Ah ! it is in such moments, when the pure and unsuspecting heart of woman is suddenly brought face to face with the falsehood, vice and wickedness of the world, when a fair and gorgeous dream of innocent life seems to rise like the elysian picture upon the curtain of a theatre, and reveal instead life's real tragedy enacted in subterranean scenes, and clothed in unearthly horrors—it is in such moments when aged, schooled and experienced vice, seems to trample upon youthful simplicity and virtue with impunity, that the courage fails, sin grows familiar, and virtue loses its elastic power of endurance.

Our faith in a higher sustaining source of strength than ourselves wavers, and with that wavering our own strength grows weak indeed. Like the young bud quickened into life by a few warm February days, and expanding—when, as its leaves begin to develop their beauty, and the serial shield which covers them parts, and the tender fibres lie open to the genial sun and warm air—if suddenly winter whitens the face of nature and withering frosts pierce again deep into the flowing sap of the forests, and down into the rivers and the soil, converting nature into a rock of ice, how quickly does that tender unfolding bud curl its blasted leaves and die, falling to the ground ; so if that delicate bud, the human soul, thus, at the very crisis of its unfolding, be surrounded by all that could freeze out its life, and chill it through and through, how shall it put forth its virtues like a green foliage, and blossom and flower as if nurtured under every favoring influence ?

The heart can only triumph over wrong when it enters upon the contest braced by the assurance that the right must ultimately triumph ; and how opposite the effect where the first lesson taught it of the difference between virtue and vice is that vice is all-powerful, and that virtue cannot resist !　There the reason acts supinely, the nerve grows feeble, and the soul drifts onward with the eddying current of circumstances.

As Ada was sitting at the little window of her cabin, on the evening of the third day after her capture, meditatively gazing out upon the ever-restless motion of the billows, and upon the calm beauty of the western sky, where the sun was now sinking into his watery couch, and drawing around him, as he departed, the cloudy glories of the firmament, Annette observed in her placid features and half-thoughtless, half-dreamy eye, that the mind of Ada had borrowed a temporary respite from sorrow.　In fact, Ada had for many hours,

at intervals, turned to listen to the chatty and viva-
cious Annette, until she had begun to imbibe certain
good-natured, submissive, try-to-be-happy impressions
which Annette had striven to console her with, and
had found a degree of pleasure and interest in her discourse, partly from the relief it afforded to the contemplation of her own misfortunes, and partly from a
growing interest in the creature whom fortune had so
singularly made her companion.

Availing herself of the favorable moment, Annette
had plied her efforts as usual, and, for this afternoon,
not unsuccessfully, to draw the desponding girl into
discourse. They had now been conversing for more
than an hour together. After a pause, in which both
seemed to be reflecting upon the topics which their
discourse had suggested, Ada turned to Annette and
said—

"Annette, you are a singular creature ! I am beginning to love you. Will you not tell me your history, and how and why I have found you where you
are ?"

"Oh," replied Annette, "I have not much of a
history. A simple girl has a few joys, little knowledge, some love, and much trouble, and you have my
history."

" But do tell me more particularly," asked Ada.

" If it will serve to wile away a tedious hour more

pleasantly to you it is at your service," replied the girl, and commenced the

STORY OF ANNETTE.

"My earliest recollections are of a gloomy old mansion in the outskirts of New Orleans. Mother I had none, but a wicked old crone, in the shape of a housekeeper, reversed the order of nature by substituting for that fostering kindness and maternal care, which are due to immortal souls just embarked in this world, the perverse malignity which could only be due to devils in the next. If I ever had an innocent wish or fancy which she did not thwart, or a guilty one which she did not encourage and endeavor to gratify, then it was because in some few instances she mistook the one for the other, and so missed her baneful intentions.

My father was an old Jew, and if my natural disposition was a medium between his and my mother's, she certainly must have been an angel, for no sooner was I old enough to entertain that assemblage of unhappy feelings called scorn, than I heartily despised him. He was rich and lent much, and the only text of Scripture which he ever knew was ' the borrower shall be servant to the lender.' The chink of money would have drawn his attention away from the sound of heavenly harps. Until I was eleven or twelve years of age, I scarce ever saw any other than these two persons. Shut up in the great gloomy prison mansion of my father, the rooms of which were seldom entered except by the old housekeeper and myself, and which were even then shrouded in twilight by the closed windows, and seeing nothing whatever of the great world around me, except what passed in the quiet back street in front of our door, or could be learned by looking out of my little bed-room window into the pent up yards and gardens in the rear of our house, I grew up to that age in as perfect ignorance of the world in which I lived, as the fluttering little canary in yonder cage of yours, Ada, is of the course we are now sailing."

"Oh, how lone !" sighed Ada. "Sister and I often thought our plantation life very lonely, but it was gaiety itself compared with your hermit home. How very dull !"

"Pardon me—I did not say it was dull. Would that I were as happy now as then !" said Annette, with a sudden emotion which for a moment choked her further utterance. "Dull ! it was the happiest portion of my life. I knew nothing ; but then I was very much happier than if I had known much, for the same reason that I often think those born blind must be happier than those who see. The most of what we see is unsightly, and pains us. It would be better if we could shut our eyes, and dream of it as all fair and beautiful. So the most that we learn is evil; but when, in our childish ignorance, we are free to dream of all things, we dream of nothing but good, and are therefore much happier."

"Time was," said Ada, "when I should have laughed at such a fancy ; but now it seems truth. But was your hermit-like retirement never broken in upon ?"

"Oh, yes. Though the house-keeper was positively forbidden to receive into the house any person whatever, yet the wily old woman, for purposes best known to herself, often relieved my loneliness by the secret and always pleasant visits of a person whom she had introduced to me as her son. Handsome and companionable, though violent and passionate—in the prime of youthful buoyancy, being a few years my senior— well studied in the world of fashion and elegance, his stolen visits were to me seasons of unalloyed bliss. From him I learned that I was beautiful ; and poor child that I was, this, with his gallantry and a kindness of manner, to which I had been a stranger, soon enabled him to learn that I loved him. Books, flowers, and music, through his unceasing attentions, and the easy opportunities afforded by the absence of my miserly old father, found their way to me, secretly, yet almost constantly. He taught me the language of each. And need I tell you that from his lips the language of them all was one which my longing and susceptible heart readily understood?

Two years had thus pleasantly and innocently ripened our attachment, when my father returned one evening from his business—where or what that might be I never knew—accompanied by a stranger.

Little as had been my knowledge of the world, from the moment I first saw that tall, polished, genteel scoundrel, I hated him from the bottom of my heart. The obsequiousness of his heartless, grey eyes was satanic. The smile had a crawling, serpent-like way of winding around his face, that made me shudder; and there was a clammy softness to his hand as he took mine, which filled me with pain. He spoke in a low, insinuating voice, and this, with his flattering manner, encouraged me after a time to tolerate him, and endeavor to overcome my first prejudices. He seemed very kind to me; and as often thenceforward as he repeated his visits, he showed me many attentions. Almost the only glimpse I ever obtained of the great world outside the little world of my birth, until I left forever that little world for that great one as my home, was when, in a reluctant compliance with his repeated request, I accompanied him to his plantation, a long way above the city. But his two daughters, of nearly my own age, of whom he had spoken to me often, and whom I longed to see, were absent at a

6

northern school, and I returned disappointed. Judge my surprise, when, after a few months of this reluctant acquaintance, my father intimated to me a desire that I should marry this Mr. Butler, for such was his name, immediately. That which before had been mere indifference, now ripened into loathing hatred. The time was fixed for my marriage, but my soul recoiled from the sinfulness of such a union, and a few days before the time of fulfillment, by a secret arrangement with my beloved Conrad, who I was not then aware was connected with the notorious Lafitte and his companions, I left the paternal threshold forever, and cast myself upon the protection of one who I was persuaded would return my confidence with a love deeper, purer, and infinitely more happifying than the paternal meanness and indifference from which I had escaped. But alas ! no long time has elapsed since I have done so, and now I fear his affections are being transferred to another object, as youthful, as beautiful, and as much my superior as yourself."

"And who is she, pray ?" inquired Ada.

" I scarcely can tell, although I have seen somewhat of her ; but ask me no more, I pray you, for this last blow to my happiness is so recent, and preys so much upon my mind, that I fear it will sadden me, and make me a dull companion to you."

CHAPTER XII.

THE PRISONERS.

"AND how?" asked Ada, when the simple narrative to which she had listened with sisterly interest had ended.

"How, Annette, can one so pure and gentle as yourself, remain in the companionship of those who are your associates here?"

"I may reply," said Annette innocently, "by inquiring how one so refined and amiable as yourself could endure to remain among such associates."

"Are you too, then, a prisoner?" asked Ada.

"I have been so long a prisoner," responded Annette, "that I have ceased to prize the story of freedom, and have learned to find pleasures and to confer happiness even in the wild and romantic sphere of life into which circumstances have thrown me. True, when I was first brought into this mode of life, I lost much time in misery, which a wiser head would have taught me might just as easily be spent in a moderate degree of happiness."

" How can you speak of the scenes you most witness as being romantic ?" asked Ada, " they seem to me to be rather wicked than romantic."

"Do not think so, dear Ada," responded Annette earnestly, "it pains me much to hear you. You must remember that you and I are of the weaker sex. Nature makes it our duty, and love renders it our pleasure only to obey. We cannot control events. That is the work of men. But wherever our lot is cast—whether amid riches or poverty, amid virtue or crime, in the quiet homes of our infancy, or out upon the wild, impressive and beautiful ocean, it is our duty to cling to man like the fruitful vine to the leafless tree, compensating by our love for his labors, and by our virtues and good qualities for his follies and faults, and the many other sources of his misery."

" You cannot possibly mean," questioned Ada proudly, " that the virtues of the female sex are to be allied to the vices of the male, so as to make up to the wicked the happiness which, by the error of their lives, they have forfeited ?"

"Not exactly that," replied Annette, " I do not hold that any woman is called upon to ally herself with aught which is beneath her morally or intellectually. Though if women ordinarily wait until they find their moral and spiritual equals among men, very few will ever love or marry. We are made by nature the purer vessels, and should exert the purifying influence over the other sex, and how can we do so unless we ally ourselves to those who are, to some extent, in need of that influence?"

"By teaching all men by our example," replied Ada, "that woman can never descend to their level, but that they must rise to woman's level before they can aspire to woman's love."

"Nobly said," returned Annette, "but before we may set them such an example, it is necessary that we should be free to set such an example as we choose. But all women are dependent—very few of them are free to do as they would. Some are controlled by fathers, brothers, owners, poverty or circumstances. We, too, are controlled, and the question with us is not whether, being in the society of pious, prayerful people, we shall voluntarily violate their wishes and our taste by descending to the companionship of the dissolute and erring—but whether, being thrown by destiny into the power of the dissolute and erring, we shall not yield to circumstances in part, and endeavor to raise up those around us more than we descend ourselves, or whether we shall—die?"

"Oh, Annette, Annette," replied Ada weeping, "I can never agree with you. And yet it seems hard, now I think of it, that such men should be utterly without love. If love is to redeem, reform and elevate, surely they most need its power.   And how shall they be expected to amend, when they are under no helping influence ?"

" Yes, gentle one," continued Annette, " and it seems to my erring imagination as though there was something beautiful in the thought that until I became a prisoner of love here, among the entire population of the wide, wide world, the influence of woman's affection was in some nobler or baser degree felt everywhere, except among this abandoned band of generous outlaws, and that when I became one of them the silken chain by which woman rules the world was complete and perfect."

Ada could not help smiling at this singular fancy, worthy of an enthusiast, and said—

" You style them generous outlaws, and I have often heard you speak of them in terms even of admiration in the same breath in which you condemn them. Pray what is there, in their conduct or profession, which entitles them to be called generous ?   I will listen to any redeeming qualities they may have, though what I have seen of them has been so fiendishly wicked, that I fear you will find me a difficult convert."

" Is it wicked or righteous to enter the homes of poor, inoffensive Africans, and tearing children from their parents, and sisters from their brothers, transport them in the diseased and deadly holds of vessels to America for slaves ?"

" A month ago," replied Ada, " I should probably have said I did not know, but now I think it is *wicked !*"

" And that such acts of wickedness can never give them a moral right or title to the property so stolen ?"

" Never !" said Ada.

" But ought not the property, the wealth accumulated by such wicked means, to grow and gather undisturbed in the hands of those who perpetrated the wickedness, so that the crimes having been successful they can flourish and fatten upon the spoils ?"

" It ought to be scattered to the four winds," answered Ada warmly, "and an avenging providence will see it done."

" But that avenging providence," continued Annette, " will employ human agents to accomplish the work, and among the most industrious and ever active of them is Lafitte."

" The wealth which he obtains is the ill-gotten proceeds of others crimes.   His profession introduces him into the company of wickedness, and he keeps company with it that he may betray it and prevent its success. He strikes the criminally wealthy to avenge the suffering and the down-trodden.   He rebukes meanness and parsimony at the points of the sabres of his followers.

He takes from the wicked what they have wrung from the unfortunate, and gives to the unfortunate what he has wrung from the wicked."

"If that be true," said Ada, "I confess to a feeling of leniency, if not admiration, for one who thus acts the part of scavenger in the moral and commercial world ; and, after all, I feel less abhorrence for the reckless brutality of those who tore me from my home, than for the cold, calculating and criminal heartlessness of my own father, who designed to sell sister Julia into my present condition. By the way, I know not but my fate is just. There seems to be a sort of systematic plan of revenge in the events which have saved my sister, and consigned myself to the fate prepared by our common parent for her. If I thought that providence designed it as just, I should submit to all its exactions and degradations with cheerfulness."

"You may rest assured that providence has controlled and will control it all," urged Annette ; "the other prisoner, of whom, by the way, I have not before spoken to you, was at first almost as despairing as yourself and I."

"Another prisoner, who and what is she pray ?"

"The other prisoner is a gentleman, Mr. Howard. He is supposed to be the owner of a large plantation, and is detained with the view of effecting a ransom. He is very unfortunate and miserable. Suddenly cut off from society and friends, he drags out a wretched prison life, as much in need of consolation and sympathy as ourselves. Poor fellow!"

"And can we not see him?" asked Ada, her heart as fully prepared to extend sympathy and relief to a worthy object, as it had been unwilling to feel the contact of one unworthy.

"Hush," whispered Annette, "if you desire to see him, though our lives would be sacrificed should it be discovered, I think I can afford you an opportunity, and I am sure that if once acquainted with him you would admire and like him, to say the least"—she continued, archly smiling, "what more two such sympathetic young companions in adversity might possibly do, I cannot even surmise."

Assuring Annette that any danger to her own life she would welcome rather than avoid, and that she could not bear to let an opportunity pass of extending her sympathy to one so deserving of it, Ada begged that she would, however, for the stranger's safety, arrange a secret and stealthy interview, and, if possible, immediately.

"I will do so," said Annette, rising.

"But wait a moment," said Ada. "Look!"

Turning, Annette beheld Ada standing before the mirror with a countenance suffused with blushes. She seemed very beautiful. Her rich folds of auburn hair fell in curls and negligent waving ringlets down by her small, well-moulded neck, upon her statue-like shoulders.   The simple though costly dress of white satin, trailed loosely and gracefully as she walked, while at the waist her fairy form, just budding into womanhood, was closely fitted and favorably shown by its neat, short bodice.   Her dress after a manner much used in the familiar or home toilet of tropical countries, was cut low in the neck, while the mere delicately ruffled band which surrounded the armpits, left revealed her graceful and tapering arms.

"Annette," said Ada, blushing, "I have consented to wear this dress when none but you were present. Do not ask me to do so on this occasion."

"My dear little prude," said Annette, laughing, we shall have to forego the opportunity of seeing him then.   For our poorly provided wardrobe contains no more Quaker-like dresses than the beautiful one you wear.   And if we wait until our arrival at the next port, it will be too late, for there I have learned Mr. Howard is to be exchanged to another vessel."

"I suppose I must submit then," said Ada, and after once more glancing in the mirror, at a costume which ill-accorded with her delicacy of taste, she sat down and awaited the arrival of the stranger, Mr. Howard.

Upon his entrance, Ada started back for a moment,

so certainly did she seem to see before her some person whom she well knew—and whom in a moment she remembered to be Mr. Defoe. But remembering, that but a few days before, she had seen him with her own eyes, shot and consigned to a watery grave— she banished the illusion, and a closer glance resolved into a mere resemblance what at first appeared as an identity. Strange and marked, however, was that resemblance, and more than once during the evening's conversation, she observed it forcibly.

The evening passed away very pleasantly, and when Mr. Howard arose to depart, Ada, sensible of the sympathy which his misfortunes had aroused in her heart, now kindled into a livelier interest by his attractive discourse and gentlemanly bearing, freely assured him that the society of one whose misfortunes were so allied to her own, would be ever welcome to her,—an invitation which Mr. Howard received with gratitude and pleasure, and promised frequently to avail himself of.

CHAPTER XIII.

THE SISTERS OF CHARITY.

" Faith, hope, and charity—these three ;
But the greatest of these is charity."

THE day had just broken over the damp and muddy streets of New Orleans, when the reverend priest and the fugitive Julia stepped through an outer gate, in a high wall enclosing a capacious yard, at the end of which stood a plain two story building, of grayish stone, moss-covered and dingy.

"Is this the house of the Sisters, holy father ?" asked Julia.

"It is, daughter," said the priest, kindly. " You will find in these hallowed precincts, if nowhere else, a place where our holy religion will guard you, and where the soul, in conscious purity and pious contemplation of divine things, may approach, as near as the veil of mortality will permit, to a vision of the rest and peace of heaven."

" How delightful," exclaimed Julia, "is such a retreat to one who is fleeing from the snares and machinations of a wicked world ! How could I but feel grateful to God and to that religion which has given me such a home !"

" Delightful, indeed !" responded the priest—" but only to a soul fitted to find delight in the things of heaven. For the pale countenances and wan forms of the Sisters whom you will see here, indicate that their lives are those of toilsome self-denial, for the good of others ; lives in which, in the eyes of the world, there is little that is delightful or attractive."

" The more attractive to me," exclaimed Julia. " For why should I not willingly flee from that world which has been to me so vile an enemy ? Why should I not freely devote the remainder of a life which has been filled to the brim with worldly happiness, and which has now nothing but degradation to hope, to the pure and holy service of Him who alone can confer true and lasting happiness ? Why should I not willingly sacrifice myself to the good of mankind—I who have been made to feel so deeply how much they are in need of every redeeming and saving influence ?"

The priest had rung several times at the door, and it was now slowly opened, though Julia saw not by whom ; and entering, she was led through the dimly lighted hall and the dark passage way into the parlor.

Here the priest, after a solemn assurance that by no possibility could her father obtain any clue to her whereabouts, left her with his blessing, and she sat down alone in the great rocking-chair, and looked at the grate of iron bars which formed one side of the apartment, and around at the simple, but elegant furniture which adorned the room, and up at the beautifully stained glass windows, just kindled into many colored hues by the rays of the rising sun. She felt alone ? No, not alone ; the folding arm of Christ seemed thrown over her, and she felt safe.

In a few moments a figure wearing the plain black gown of a Sister of Charity, with long cape, and a white cap partially concealing her thin, pallid face, stood within the door, bearing in her hand a small lamp. Without raising her eyes from the floor, or speaking, she slightly beckoned to Julia to follow her, with which sign Julia complied ; and after passing along several narrow corridors, and up a flight of stairs, she placed the lamp upon a table in a small, neatly furnished apartment, and as noiselessly retired. Julia gazed for a moment earnestly and interestedly after the mute figure of her who seemed thus to walk through earth, with her thoughts not even for a moment withdrawn from heaven ; and after repeating her accustomed prayers, retired to that repose of which she stood so much in need.

CHAPTER XIV.

JULIA, A POSTULANT.

> No feverish cares to that divine retreat
> Thy woman's heart of silent worship brought;
> ut a fresh childhood, heavenly truth to meet
> With love, and wonder, and submissive thought."
>
> MOORE.

DURING those intervals of Julia's early life which had been spent away from Lindenhall, not the least pleasing of the opportunities attending the change of scene, were those of attending upon public worship in the cathedrals of the Church of Rome. Her poetic imagination was charmed, and her love of the mystic and incomprehensible gratified by the imposing symbolic ceremonies which there constantly passed before her.

The flock where the highest and the lowest of society seemed to bow in confessed equality before God, kneeling reverently in the humble posture of worship, with the emblem of their Saviour's suffering before them—the holy stillness which rested over the congregation—now broken by the soft, deep tones of the organ, as they wandered among the columns, and echoed from the vaulted roof of the sombre cathedral, accompanied, perhaps, by a single delicate female voice, which one moment swells upon the ear with a rich harmonious fullness, and the next dies away upon the heart, soft as the sigh of an Æolian harp, and anon deepens into the full chorus of congregational praise—the mute language of worship of the priests, whom she so much revered—the majesty and sonorous beauty of the unknown tongue in which the nations of such varied languages and kindred unite in chanting the same praises to their common Father—the costume and genuflections of the assistants before the altar—the altar itself, with its beautiful image of the crucifixion and of the loved Virgin, decorated with ever-fragrant flowers, and lit by a thousand tapers— all of this mute typical language of the soul charmed her with the sensible majesty of the cross and the beauty of holiness.

Upon the incense that rose before the altar, she breathed her prayers, confident that that ascending mist would bear them to heaven, there to unite with those that curtain the glories of the Father.

At times, entranced in a delightful rapture of adoration and delight, she would find herself kneeling in her place after the congregation had dispersed. Upon one of these occasions, a venerable father, whose grey-haired age filled her with reverence, had spoken to her so kindly and earnestly of the dangers by which she was beset in a world of wickedness, and gave her incidentally so touching and pleasing a picture of the quiet and happy foretaste of heaven which those enjoy who devote their entire selves to the service of God, that from that moment the whole vista of life to her wore a less dazzling, and more subdued brightness. Though she had no thought of devoting herself to such a life, yet it occurred to her that had she been differently situated, with no father whom it was her duty to comfort and make happy, and no gentle sister Ada whom she could guide, enjoy, and love, or should these be taken from her, the life of a *religeuse* would have seemed to her a congenial duty.

And now, that she had discovered for the first time the calamity into which she was borne, and which at once deprived her of her father and sister, and even of herself, and took from her the most sacred of all rights—the right to be pure and holy—she felt a thrilling consciousness of her right to be the servant of God rather than of man.

In this calamity, the same holy father whose conversations in the chapel had so deeply impressed her, had come to her as we have seen—had revealed to her her misfortune, and had afforded her her chosen refuge within the enfolding and protecting arm of the church.

The dream, upon which she had pondered, now seemed the mirrored reflection of her future, and she entered without misgivings, but with a heart full of gratitude and serene joy, into an institution where she hoped soon to put on not only the modest habit, but the benevolent life of a Sister of Charity. Another motive afforded her an additional inducement.

In her infancy, when in the city, she had heard from common rumor of the devoted Sister Clara, whose never-tiring benevolence was the theme of many, and of whom Father Reilly had spoken often as one of whom even the church might be proud.

This holy woman, as Julia had now learned, was her mother. When she thought of this, she could almost, in anticipation, smile at the cruel stroke which had deprived her of father and sister. She hoped soon to meet, and, as she trusted, to embrace, in the double fullness of religious and natural affection, this divine woman.

When she·arose the next morning, however, and went down to ask permission of the mother superior to do so, she was informed that Sister Clara had left the house before the dawn, upon her daily routine of charity, from which she would not return until late.

" Besides," said the mother superior, in a mild and benign tone, which contrasted strangely, as Julia thought, with the severity of the unexpected restriction laid upon her, " besides, daughter, you enter to-day upon the preparation for a life in which the natural and sinful affections of this world are to be replaced by purer and holier attachments to the things of another world. Christ must be your father, the holy virgin your mother, and we your sisters. That you may enter upon your novitiate by putting away all worldly and sinful affections, rather than by fostering new hindrances to the perfect loves of religion, I shall direct that you may not see Sister Clara until all tendencies towards that worldly affection with which alone you, as a child after the flesh, regard her, shall have been subdued as an unworthy and sinful lust. You may then meet her with the same, and no other affection, than that which you would feel for any other member of the sisterhood."

This fell upon Julia like a heavy blow where a kiss was expected, but a moment's thought convinced, or partially convinced, her of its propriety, and she returned to her room to meditate, and, after a few moments, to weep. How little she expected that such would be her feelings upon the first morning of her life as a postulant.

CHAPTER XV.

SYMPATHY.

"Come, chase that starting tear away,
　　Ere mine to meet it springs ;
To-night, at least, to-night be gay,
　　Whate'er to-morrow brings.
Like sunset gleams, that linger late
　　When all is dark'ning fast,
Are hours like these we snatch from Fate—
　　The brightest and the last."　　　　MOORE.

WITH each ensuing day Ada found a more and more welcome relief from the sense of her own misfortunes in the company of Mr. Howard, and she did not wonder that a person so social, and who had been so long compelled to commune only with his own melancholy thoughts, should gladly avail himself of every opportunity to enjoy her society. The prisoner seemed to have ingratiated himself but little into the acquaintance of Annette, and, as for the other persons on board, neither herself, nor, so far as she could learn, Mr. Howard, were ever made aware of their presence, except by hearing occasionally the harsh word of command, or tramp of feet upon deck.

It was, therefore, with little surprise and no displeasure, that Ada, as she often sat silently gazing out of one of the little stern windows which lighted her *boudoir*, and thinking dreamily or sadly of other days, would hear the light tap of her fellow-captive upon the door, and rising, with a hasty glance at the mirror, and a hurried arrangement of some wandering curl, would lift the latch and receive him with a pleased and familiar smile.

Nor would the reason have been difficult to guess. An easy flow of pleasant imaginative thought seeming ever to inspire him, was mingled with occasional involuntary outbursts of bold energy which made her tremble, yet attracted her. His heart-felt expressions of interest in her safety, and the thousand little devices and ingenious schemes which he would suggest for her rescue, and the many reasons he would sanguinely urge, for the belief that they were soon to be rescued without harm, from the position of fear and danger in which they were placed, cheered her spirits and called forth her gratitude, at least for that friendly desire which was father to his faith.

Sometimes during these visits, he would wile away the hours by reading to her in a low, soft, agreeable voice, from such authors as the little library of her cabin, or his own trunk could furnish, or in narrating some of the wild and thrilling adventures through which he had passed while upon one of the American privateers in the still pending war with England.

In return for this kindness, Ada told him freely of the trivial joys and sorrows of her bird-like infancy, her school days and all her life up to the moment they had met, to which he would listen with ravished interest.

To this pleasant interchange of thought, Annette, in whom Ada's interest had much diminished in the more attractive society of Mr. Howard, though always present, became less and less a party, until Mr. Howard and Ada both began to feel that her society was rather a restraint than a pleasure to them. Still those hours, sweetened by the thought that, as if providentially, they had been permitted to cull them like flowers from among the thorns of misfortune, relieved the anguish of Ada, and seemed to turn her life into a tolerable and even agreeable portion.

Often after Howard had returned to his room, or rather cell, from which a narrow passage way led by the rooms of Ada and Annette, she would gaze long and fixedly at the closed door, and wonder that any person could so soon have so fully enlisted her sympathy as to make her so forget her own misfortunes. Of his life, except the few detached adventures and exploits of his recent career, she knew almost nothing. His strange resemblance to the arch-villain Defoe sometimes flashed painfully across her mind, but she no longer felt surprised that her sister had been induced to love one who resembled so admirable a person as Howard.

Several weeks had thus passed. It was the afternoon of a beautiful summer's day. The sun was shining warmly down upon the calm, unruffled waters of the gulf, and the vessel slept motionless upon her native element. Ada was sitting in her accustomed place by the window, looking out upon the boundless waves, and musing. Annette was reclining upon a small sofa, beautifully carved of rosewood, and richly cushioned. A Persian tissue of a tasteful pattern yielded to their fairy footsteps. Rich satin curtains, softened by overlying folds of gauze, hung in graceful folds on every side, and shut out of view the fact that this was not only a *boudoir*, but a sleeping apartment. A guitar, and two or three ebony chairs, with brocatelle cushions, furnished the room. Here and there, from behind the curtains, appeared glimpses of paintings which a critic would have attributed to the studio of some of his admired masters. A golden chandelier of fairy proportions suspended its tiny waxen tapers in the centre of the room, while a large mirror, suspended upon the farther side, twinned by its reflection the magic beauty of this little *boudoir* of taste and luxury.

Step by step, yielding to the persuasions of Annette, Ada had suffered herself to be attired not as became a captive, but rather as befitted the queen of her little fairy dominion. Annette herself was prettily attired in a gown of snowy white, bound at the waist by a belt of scarlet velvet, held in front by a small silver clasp. Her dark eyes were veiled by long curling lashes, and her comely features, moulded after the peculiar cast of Jewish female beauty, were shaded by folds of her rich, luxuriant hair, that fell in graceful though negligent curls below her waist.

With this simplicity, the attire of Ada contrasted. Low over her shoulders fell her gown of purple satin, united at the waist by a belt of plain black velvet and a heavy gold clasp. Peeping out from under the gown the folds of an underdress of gauze, swept over the graceful contour of her bosom, and were joined nearly down to the waist by a broach, richly studded with brilliants, which gleamed forth from the witching recess in which they were embowered, faintly yet interestingly as stars in mid-day. Just above this a delicate chemisette spanned across and cast its shadow, curved like cupid's bended bow, upon her full bosom. There also reposed the image of the Saviour, enwrought in ivory upon a plain, large golden cross, suspended by a necklace of pearls, that rose and fell with her frequent sighs. From its confinement, the skirts parted, revealing her richly embroidered under-dress of white muslin, from beneath which the toe of her tiny moccasin witchingly protruded. Her hair was confined only by a pretty band or coronet, which crossed her brows, in the centre of which a diamond of unusual brilliancy glistened like a star. Escaping thence, her golden hair, in a flood of irregular tresses rather than curls, sweeping by her meek, confiding eyes of heavenly blue, fell upon her shoulders, and across her bosom and down in luxuriant exuberance among the folds of her skirts, as a pearling mountain stream pitches from its topmost height, and dividing in its course, reaches by many channels the base of the beautiful precipice over which it loves to leap.

Powerful as was the charm of her beauty, so expressive of the inner loveliness of her character, it had borrowed additional potency from the faultless taste of Annette, who had arrayed it as for the bridal, and to whose taste Ada had to-day, for the first time, yielded all her past scruples. No wonder that as Mr. Howard entered soon after, it was with a flutter of admiration, and that as he took the quivering hand of Ada, his hand also trembled.

" I think," said Mr. Howard, seating himself by her side, " the air of the sea more than compensates, in its effects upon your health, for the close confinement to which your are subject. Truly, I never saw you looking so well."

" I am very well," replied Ada. " Indeed, since my first pangs of despair have subsided, and especially since my captivity has been releaved by Annette's attentions and your kind society, I have been quite cheerful, though I often wish I could enjoy both under more favorable circumstances."

" Annette is a pattern of philosophical wisdom," replied Mr. Howard, deferentially. "I know not what I would have done but for her cheering presence to teach me the difficult art of picking roses from the briars."

" Yes," said Annette, " my maxim is that what is to be will be, and therefore that whatever is, is right. Hence there is no use to try to sail against wind and .ide. The best way is to float with both and we will find it easy rowing for a while at least. For my part I cannot think that any of us would suffer much if we were only ready and willing to enjoy what we could. But, alas ! my philosophy happens at this moment to be overturned by my experience, for I have such a violent headache, I shall not be able to enjoy your company. Will you excuse me, dearest Ada ?" she asked, faintly, as she rose to retire.

" Oh, Annette, I am very sorry you cannot be with us," said Ada, with a slight tremor at the thought of being left alone with Mr. Howard, though she had often secretly wished it.

"I hope Miss Annette will try to be with us. Ada is so well, and will be so lively this afternoon. I am sure you will quite forget your illness presently," smiled Mr. Howard.

"I am very sorry," said Annette. "I had hoped to enjoy the afternoon very much, but you know, Ada, my head has been aching for several hours. I hope you will excuse me."

"Oh, certainly," said Ada, "if we must," kissing her as they parted at the door.

"Certainly," said Mr. Howard, with his fingers upon the latch.

The door closed, and Mr. Howard conducted Ada to the sofa. Never had she, in the presence of any person, felt such a consciousness of her own weakness as then. That Mr. Howard was in every way her superior, she did not doubt. There was something in his calm, earnest, self-dependent manner, as well as in the energy and intensity of his intellect, which had ever overawed and impressed her, and which, at that moment, made her feel as if she needed some supporting prop to rest upon. So sensibly was she impressed with this feeling of weakness that she could scarcely have resumed the conversation, but Mr. Howard relieved her by saying——

"Annette is a good creature, though her life has, in some respects, been unfortunate."

"I pity and love her," replied Ada.

"Her errors were those of a pure heart, and I should admire much more that gentle portion of her sisterhood, who loved and pitied, than that which condemned her."

Ada blushed and remained silent.

"Youth is the turning point of life," pursued her visitor. "Ah! with what sad reflections do I look back upon mine."

"Sad!" said Ada, tenderly, lifting her long silken lashes from their downcast droop, and resting her moistened eyes upon his. "Your youth can scarcely yet be said to be past. But I thought it was very happy."

"Some portions of it were," he replied, "but at the last it was blighted—witheringly blasted, and has been miserable ever since."

"By what affliction," asked Ada, involuntarily leaning forward in her interest, and suffering her tiny hand to repose upon his own.

"By the heaviest of all afflictions—love," replied Mr. Howard, smiling.

Ada relapsed into her former position with a coquettish frown of pleased disappointment.

"Why, Mr. Howard, I supposed you were proof against such calamities."

"Since that time I have endeavored to be ; but every day convinces me how hard it is to keep my resolution."

"You certainly could not be placed in better circumstances for keeping it than here, away from that society in which alone you could be won to break it," said Ada, playing childishly with the twining tresses of golden hair which strayed across her lap.

"Perhaps so," he replied, carelessly. "What a noble vessel is now crossing so near our wake," said he, passing one arm over her snowy shoulders, while with the other he pointed out the approaching object.

"Yes," said Ada, turning, and leaning upon the familiar arm that she might see it better. "It is so seldom they cross our path, that their presence seems very, very welcome. Ah ! how I wish you knew whom you were approaching, and would try to capture her."

"I am sure I would do so with pleasure, did I see the possibility of success," replied Mr. Howard, with a smile."

"You ! Why, Mr. Howard, of course you could do nothing. I was talking to the vessel."

"Oh ! I beg pardon."

"Alas !" she continued, turning from the vessel and gazing into his warm, flashing eye, with innocent simplicity, "in that matter I fear neither of us can assist the other much. Now, Mr. Howard—there, never mind your arm ; I did not change my position because it was unpleasant to me—I prefer you should act with the freedom of a brother with one towards whom you have been so brotherly. Now, I have a favor to beg. Will you not tell me all about the sad affection which has rested like a blight over your happiness ? You know it is an interest deeper than mere curiosity which leads me to ask it."

"It is a painful, though brief story, which I have never told to living mortal before," he said, "and which I should prefer never to tell to you, as it involves the prevalent charge against one of your sex. At least, you will permit me to defer it to some other time."

"Ah ! Mr. Howard, another time we may never see together. Do pray tell me, that I may sympathize in your sorrow."

"And avoid," suggested Mr. Howard, smiling, "the same error of inconstancy, which has so often converted love from the richest of blessings into the deadliest of poisons. For the last consideration, if you will accept it, I will give you the brief, though to me affecting narrative.

"Deeply and permanently associated with the earliest recollections of my infancy," he commenced, "is the image of Ellen Melrose. The humble homes of our parents were closely adjoining, and in a district in which there were no other neighbors for many miles. My first recollections of her tiny little form are when we would meet at the garden fence, which bounded her father's garden from that of my mother, and there spend hours in quiet, child-like communion, before we were yet able to talk even to each other. As we grew older, our companionship, though as free of guile and more intelligent, was not less intimate. At play, at school—everywhere but at the table and in sleep—we were constantly together, until she was thirteen years of age. Then she began to be less familiar, and finally became quite demure and shy, but still very kind, very winning, very pretty. I loved her the more for the feminine, lady-like modesty which grew upon her; and though then we could not romp wildly together as before, our walks were more seldom, and more staid and quiet, and never continued far from her house; and though I was obliged to change my old manner of testifying my regard for her by open words, or by a hearty kiss, and instead to present her a wild flower, or a little tame rabbit, or a dove, or something of that description, yet I felt such a propriety and beauty in all this, which without a word of reproof or correction she mysteriously impressed upon me, that in a word I was fully and fairly in love.

"I was not long in making my heart known to her.

At first, she fluttered modestly, like a timid bird when first caught, but soon, as if by a decree of our natures which neither of us could resist, the perfect confidence of our infancy was fully restored, heightened by a more powerful and tender attachment, which appeared to me to borrow a softer, deeper, and lovelier hue as we watched together each succeeding sunset."

"How happy !" remarked Ada, as her dreamy eyes seemed to gaze upon the picture of unallowed affection.

"Those were indeed sweet and happy moments," continued Mr. Howard. "Were I persuaded that earth could ever renew them for me, I should be fully content to endure all the evils of life with buoyant hope."

"And have you no hope that earth can renew them ?" asked Ada.

"Alas !" said Mr. Howard, "would that it might! But such affection is a mellow fruit, that ripens only in the sunshine of implicit confidence ; and I fear that my subsequent experience has so corroded my heart with distrust, that I am scarcely worthy of the love of one so unselfish and angelic as I once supposed Ellen Melrose to be."

Ada sighed, and said nothing, but the soft, heavenly light of her blue orbs rested upon his dark, earnest eye with an expression of unmingled sympathy, which he seemed not to notice, as his thoughts were entirely fixed upon the distant object of which he was speaking, but which, with the occasional sudden heaving and falling of the crucifix upon her bosom, revealed more of the heart than either seemed to be aware of.

" So," he continued, " our lives down to the age of seventeen glided smoothly into each other, like two pearly brooks which have met in one, to be divided no more forever. Then I was obliged to choose a profession, and having an uncle in the command of an East India merchantman, with whom my mother was quite desirous to place me, thinking that a few years of faithful attendance to my duties would raise me to some responsible and lucrative command, I determined to go to sea. I need not tell you how my betrothed, who, I believe, verily thought she loved me as heart never before loved, wept and sobbed when I broke to her the news, that for the first time in our lives we were to be separated, and that, too, for a very, very long time, for two, or even three years, at the end of which time I hoped to have the command of a similar vessel, and then to claim her as my own and make her my bride. She urged me by all that was good, or could excite my pity, not to go where I should be obliged to leave her alone so long. Poor fool that I was, that I did not listen to her," groaned Howard, as for a moment he covered his face with his handkerchief, while his manly frame shook with emotion.

As he removed the covering from his face, and turned again to Ada to resume his story, her downcast eyes reverted from him to the floor. They were suffused with tears—several large drops of the pure dew of sympathy lingered upon her cheeks, and one had fallen upon her bosom, which ever and anon heaved convulsively.

" I perceive," he continued, " my dear young friend, that your warm, sympathetic heart is grieved, rather than interested, by my story, and I will close the curtain upon it now, for the rest is all—all dark. The ship was gone nearly three years."

" It was difficult for us to send letters, many of them miscarried, and their answers were long in coming. Besides, my port was changed so that but one or two of her letters reached me. Feeling sick at heart whenever I sat down to write, at the thought that the whole world lay between us, and that the answer to my letter could not by possibility reach me within a year, and probably would not at all, I trusted my love to her constancy, and wrote but seldom. At the end of three years I returned to that lonely hamlet among the hills. Faint rumors had reached home of my death, but I knew they were not such as truthful love would recognize. As the two cottages, in which she and I had lived and loved away the sunshiny morning of life, came to view, my bursting heart seemed as if it would tear my feet from the earth, and bear me onward upon hidden wings. I ran like a deer, and wept like a child. There they were, the consecrated scenes of my infancy and my love. I felt faint and sick, so overcome was I with emotions of gratitude, that I had been spared from the fearful tempests, and all the dangers of war and the deep, to return now and behold the cot of her infancy and mine, still the same, not a tree removed, not a picket changed, not a flower more or less than when I left it, that I involuntarily sunk upon the sod and said, 'Heavenly Father! all this I have not deserved. Oh, God, I thank thee!' Again I arose and ran on, across the heath and over the meadows, as when a boy. My heart was in a bursting storm of excitement. 'Where was *she?*' thought I, 'and why had she not come out to meet me? Alas,' I thought, 'she does not know of my coming, or she would have met me with the pilot that brought us into harbor. But so much the greater will be her joy when I shall clasp her, after my long absence, to my bosom.' My mother's door was nearest. I saw her aged form, more bowed, I thought, than when I had last seen it come tottering out over the threshold. But I could not stop. With the speed of the wind I rushed past. I stood at the door of

Ellen. I lifted the latch and entered. The room was deserted. A moment sufficed for me to dart over the house, through every room, but all was deserted and still. Full of a thousand forebodings, I returned to the house of my mother. The clear bell of the neighboring village church chimed merrily forth, as it had done in the hours of my childhood. After the first joyful embraces were over, I begged of her to tell me where Ellen was. But my poor old mother, as the words fell from me, put her thin fingers upon my lips, and laid her head upon my broad breast, now struggling with every conflicting emotion, and weeping, said—

" 'Forgive her, my poor boy, forgive her, for she meant not wrong. But yonder chiming bells have just ceased, and now Ellen Melrose is standing before the altar to be married. All the people of the village have gone to see her, for all say she will be the most beautiful bride who has ever stood before that altar. I alone remained at home, for I knew that on earth or in heaven, she was plighted to my poor Arthur, my boy far off on the ocean, and I could not see her given to a stranger. God have mercy on you, my poor boy, and help you to forget her.'

" As my mother repeated over and over again her weeping wish, she led my tottering form to a chair, for I could not stand. My head sunk upon my bosom, I thought I could feel that the throbbings of my heart were growing less and less frequent, and I believed and hoped that I was dying. I passed off into a sort of lethargic dream, in which I saw over and over again her hand given to another, and her sweet smile as she bowed when asked ' to love, honor and obey' a stranger. I remembered no more until I awoke the next morning.

"Then my mother informed me that at the wedding thrice had the beautiful bride stood up to yield to the ceremony, and thrice she had been obliged, by sudden illness, to resume her seat,—that strange visions of fear seemed to pass every moment before her, and that her wedding had been a memorably sad affair to all who had witnessed it. Then, Ada, I knew that Ellen Melrose had loved me still, even while she had vowed to love another ; but, alas, what pleasure could I find in so doubly wretched a thought. I never saw her again, but left my mother's house in a few hours, to which I have never returned, but whither I was about returning when I was taken prisoner by this vessel, and I know not now whether I may ever again visit the home of my infancy."

" Ah !" cried Ada, as he ceased the narrative, " how I pity poor, poor Ellen."

" Ellen ?" inquired Howard with surprise.

" Yes," replied Ada. " You have no consciousness of vows broken, or of tender affections blighted by

your fault. The history of your love has been that of
a noble struggle on your part to bless and make happy
the object loved. On hers, it must remind her painfully, that while you were engaged for her sake in this
noble struggle, her inconstancy and fickleness has
blasted her happiness forever. She has fallen from a
position so many would have envied, to that of being
bound eternally to one she does not love, while you
are free to centre your affections upon some more constant object if you can ever meet with one worthy of
your regard."

As the beautiful Ada closed this sentence with a
trembling voice and hesitating manner, evidently too
much absorbed by her sympathies to be fully conscious
of the import of her words, and then blushed as if
fearful she might have expressed too much, Mr. Howard for the first time placed her hand in his, and for a
moment gazed upon her trembling, lovely form, and
steadily and passionately into her suffused and lustrous
eyes. How could he but read that the artless young
creature before him was sweetly and confidingly throbbing with a love whose nature and intensity she in her
simplicity had not paused to fathom, and which could
he otherwise than return ?

In another moment he knelt before her, and bowed
his lips to the tiny, trembling hand of Ada, which in-

voluntarily unfolded to receive their pressure, like a flower at the kiss of the sun.

"Can I—dare I hope," he murmured faulteringly, "that the one person who in every feature and lineament is the image of the once loved Ellen, and who has called forth the boundless passion of a heart which I had thought never could love again—can you, dearest Ada, permit me to hope ——"

A slight, warm pressure from the soft and fairy hand which rested upon his, seemed to course his veins with a thrill of lightning, for it told him all a lover could have asked. The other fell from the blushing brows it had shaded down to her lap, as if invitingly tendering him its fairy strength to lift him up from his kneeling position. A sweet smile wreathed her lips, which as he rose, now emboldened to press them, he saw gathered into a bewitching readiness to receive his own. They met, and still lingered and clung together with a soft and delightful pressure.— Transported in a whirl of happy sensations, Ada sunk languidly reclining upon his arm. Tenderly he clasped her yielding form. Her arms involuntarily rose to enfold the object of her love in their embrace, while in the confusion of her thoughts she could but murmur, in a broken whisper—

"Let me be to you as Ellen. Nay, as Ruth to Naomi : 'Entreat me not to leave thee, or to return from following after thee ; for whither thou goest I will go, and where thou lodgest I will lodge ; thy people shall be my people, and thy God my God.'— Ah, dearest, never till now had I learned how sweet was the cup of love."

At that moment the dream of passion into which they were passing was broken by a light rap at the door, and Annette entered, bearing a lamp, for it was now growing twilight. Lighting with it several of the miniature tapers of the chandelier, and requesting Ada to watch it and light others, as they would soon burn out and leave them in darkness, she again excused herself on account of her violent head ache, and left Mr. Howard and Ada to themselves.

CHAPTER XVI.

"IASAACKS."

"Here lurked a wretch who had not crept abroad
　　For forty years—no face of mortal seen:
In chamber brooding like a loathly toad;
　　And sure his linen was not very clean.
Through secret loop-holes that had practised been,
　　Near to his bed, his dinner vile he took;
Unkempt and rough, of squalid face and mien—
　　Our castle's shame!"　　　　CASTLE OF INDOLENCE.

VERY early that morning, habited in her usual garb of gray, with long cape, and a bonnet that nearly concealed her features—now pale almost to transparency, yet still beautiful, notwithstanding the disease which had marked them, and soft and winning in their expression—Sister Clara might have been seen issuing with her usually quick, though delicate step, from the threshold of the house of the sisterhood, and through the heavy iron gate into the street. The dawn had just broken, and the lamps were not yet extinguished. The countenance of Sister Clara beamed with the holiness and charity of her vocation, and would have gone farther towards converting the unbeliever to a faith in the institution to which she was attached, than volumes of argument.   Her eyes, though very black, large, and lustrous, were now more subdued, perhaps, than in their youth, and beamed with an expression of exceeding kindness and benevolence, softened by a shade of sadness.   Her complexion had never been removed from the pure Circassian by a shade sufficient to hide the rose upon her cheek, though now that rose had vanished, and was replaced usually by a lily-like paleness, occasionally substituted by the hectic flush of the consumptive.   Here and there a delicate wrinkle marked the footsteps of time, or the traces of deeper destroyers upon her countenance.   And as she paused a moment in front of the gate, as if hesitating which route to pursue, the slightly chilly air even of that August morning, went painfully to her lungs, and she coughed with a deep, hollow, and fearful sound, which seemed to say that she was more fit to receive than to give the nursing and healing attentions of a Sister of Charity.

In a moment she took the street which led to the left from the institution, and seeming at every turn to avoid the more respectable thoroughfares, she came at length into one of the lowest streets, or rather alleys of the city.

The buildings—old and wooden—were nearly all of one story, none of them more than two—unpainted, rudely patched, black, reeling, and dilapidated—and occupied almost entirely as liquor stalls and junk shops. Into the narrow street were now skulking or emerging a population corresponding to the locality—ragged, besotted, and bruised—mostly negroes or whites of the grossest appearance—with pitiable and brutal faces, expressive only of poverty, crime, and misery.

The Sister pursued her way as if habituated to the scene around her, until by a narrow doorway, the door of which hung suspended upon one hinge, and which she had some difficulty in removing, she passed into a still narrower passage, the paved floor of which seemed to have been used rather as a sewer for refuse, slops and filth than as an alley, and by this reached a small yard, indescribably filthy, at the further end of which was a more commodious rear house, which might once have been respectable in appearance. Its doors and shutters were fastened, and the moss grew over its threshold and window-sills, as if it had been asleep for a century.

Drawing a bunch of keys from her pocket, Sister Clara noiselessly applied one of them to the door. It opened, and she as noiselessly entered into a hall, in which, as she closed the door, the faint morning light which came in through a few panes over the door, partially covered with green paper, scarcely relieved the darkness. An open door, however, led into a parlor, better lighted by a hole in a broken window-blind, beneath which was a broken pane, as if some heavy missil had been thrown through. A shattered chandelier stood upon the mantel-piece, beneath which were its fragments of glass, and in one corner of the room lay a heavy paving stone. With these exceptions, the neat antique furniture of the room appropriate to the parlor of a person in medium circumstances, corresponded with the outward appearance of the house, and looked as if it might have slept there in undisturbed repose for half a century. Through the great hole in the window-blind and pane, the dust had entered, and lay beneath it like a snow-drift upon the floor. A chair that sat in its way, had caught its due share of the descending cloud ; and upon every article of furniture the undisturbed film of dust, here and there relieved by the web of the house spider, indicated that no housewife or other meddling person had there intruded for many years.

We have said that she entered the hall in silence : not so. Hardly had the door closed upon her, when a springing and creaking sound, as if a lunatic were turning a somerset upon a rickety bedstead, was heard, and at her first step along the hall she stopped, and involuntarily quaked for a moment, as a weird, shrill, piping voice shrieked rapidly from beneath—

" Who's there ? who's there ? who's there ?"

Without immediately answering, she again proceeded, stepping cautiously down the dark stairs, in the direction of the voice, which came from the rear of the house, and apparently from the cellar.

"Who's there? Robbers! thieves!" shrieked the voice fearfully, and in accents of almost maniac earnestness. "I've got nothing; go away; don't come here; Iasaaks is poor! Who are you? Who's there, I say?"

"Sister Clara," responded the holy nun, in a voice which seemed for a moment to abate his insane anxiety.

"Sister Clara! Ah, yes—quick—let me see you. Where's my child? Have you brought her? Have you found her?" And then, as she crept stealthily along the dark passage, she heard his high, shrill voice, as he again piped forth, between a yell and a whisper—

"I don't believe it—it's a cheat! Sister Clara? No! robbers—robbers! I tell you, don't come here!' And again the springing sound came, and the bed creaked awfully. At length she reached the door from whence these fearful, incoherent ravings still issued, and opened it.

The room was very dark—lit only like the parlor by two similar holes in the broken shutter and pane. The air was earthly damp and offensive. The apartment was quite large but almost naked of furniture. A few broken chairs and three or four chests were arranged along the sides of the room, and scattered over the floor, which was of earth, trodden to hardness. The walls were of brick and stone. In the farther and darker corner of this cellar, bolt upright upon a rude, bare, unpillowed bed, thin and formed of straw, sat a shrivelled figure, covered to the waist only with its soiled linen, and inadequately concealed as to the remainder by the remnant of a sheet and an old blanket.

As she entered he withdrew his shading hand from above his peering eyes and revealed a gaunt face, which might have been copied by Hogarth as the picture of famine. A few white hairs formed a sort of beard, running around the back of his head from ear to ear. The rest of his small, low cranium was entirely bare. He had no forehead, but the top of his head commenced at the root of his great heavy nose and run backward and upward. His small, snake-like eyes emitting a wild maniac glare, by which they seemed to have looked themselves into blindness, were far apart, and his head immediately behind them broad. His mouth was small and gathered into a whirlpool of wrinkles, which also formed two minor eddys around his eyes. His chin was almost wanting, and his cheeks sunken, so that his whole face seemed merged into one gigantic feature—the nose. Here and there a single penurious, stinted hair, of several inches in length, strayed over his countenance, like the long effort of some seed sprouting towards the light in a dark cellar, but he had no beard. Beside him upon his bed, and with one of his arms resting upon it, lay a plain open coffin, the lid of which was leaning against the wall behind him. A part of another chest appeared from beneath his bed ; upon the end of which were a tin cup of water and a broken remnant of bread. There was no fireplace in the apartment. It was a bare cellar.

"Have you found her ?" exclaimed this frightful apparition, eagerly, as she entered. "Do you bring my daughter ? Speak, woman !"

Sister Clara shook her head, and advancing, took from the basket which she carried under her arm, a portion of a loaf of bread.

"Have you heard nothing from her ?" he continued.

"Nothing whatever," said Sister Clara.

"Away—away—then, you harlot," raved the drawling lunatic. "What do you come here for ? You come here to find me dead, so that you can get my money. I've got no money. Iasaacks is poor. There, give me that bread."

She cut him off a piece and watched him while he ate it.

"If it were not for you I'd starve. But it's not charity that brings you here. If I waited for that I'd starve too. You think I've got money, and that I'll turn Christian and leave it to you. I want you to think so—but I won't. I'll not leave the worship of my fathers. Besides, I've got no money. Don't I tell you I'm poor, you miserable shrew ? Don't I tell you ——

"Give me the whole of that bread. Why not ? do you think I'll hide it, and not eat it ? What a fool ! Iasaacks is poor. Iasaacks is hungry—but Iasaacks is poor, and can't buy anything to eat. It's very kind in you to come and feed him," muttered the old chatterer as he rapidly devoured piece after piece of the victual she had brought—"for you know Iasaacks is very poor and would starve. Yet people that don't know him say he's got money. Where, I'd like to know ? In these chests ? Ha ! ha ! Here are the keys—there they are—take them. You may have all you can find. No secret drawers—no springs—and, ha ! ha ! no money. Why should there be ? Iasaacks is poor—Iasaacks is poor."

"Now," said Sister Clara, in a tone whose mild, soothing gentleness contrasted strangely with that of the shattered being before her, " now take this cup of water. It will cool your heated brows, and do you good. Our religion teaches us that to give a cup of—"

"Fire and brimstone ! D—— your religion," shrieked the man, with one hand gesturing wildly in the violence of his passion, and with the other eagerly snatching the cooling cup. " You can't convert me," said he, pausing for a moment to drink spasmodically. " Make an apostate renegade of me ! I follow the faith of my fathers. There, leave me this piece for my supper. You won't leave me to starve, will you ? You who expect to get all I'm worth—which is nothing ! There, that's right," said he, seizing the remnant of bread she gave him.

" Now I've got enough of you—clear out. Do you want to stop and eat up yourself this miserable morsel which will just barely last me till I die ? Yes ! you'd like to, and leave me to starve. You pretend you are trying to find my daughter. Poor Annette ! poor Annette ! But you're not—you witch—you hag. You're deceiving me. Now," said he, raising his voice as the holy sister prepared to retire, flinging aloft his arms, and flourishing his clenched fists in a manner that would have been frightful to one of less nerve than Sister Clara. " Now—do you hear me ? I've had enough of your hypocritical charity. You come here to eat out my substance. Clear out—begone, you wretch—begone—begone !"

She closed the door. Scarcely had she done so, when he tottered to the floor, and lifting the lid of the chest which protruded from beneath his bed, exposing its contents, consisting of decaying scraps of

bread and other filthy food, which he had received and
saved in the same manner, he thrust the portion she
had left with him, into the offensive receptacle, and
closing the lid quickly, fell once more hurriedly upon
the couch, turned towards the door and listened to the
receding footsteps of the saint, until she had emerged
into the yard, and then placing one of his fingers beside his nose, and with those of the other hand rap-
ping a hollow tune upon his coffin—he, still sitting upright on his bed, stared against the vacant wall, and
grinned horribly, then threw off his covering, jumped
into his coffin, and laid down.

CHAPTER XVII.

THE PRISONER.

Daniel.—" Quot homines tot sententiæ."
Martin.—" And what is that ?"
Daniel.—" 'Tis Greek, and argues difference of opinion."
JOHN WOODVILLE.

THE sun had risen, and industrious people and slaves were entering upon the business of the day, and aristocrats and vagabonds were just gliding off into their second nap, when Sister Clara emerged from the dingy passage leading to the house of the Jew, into the scarcely less dingy street. The vagabonds being almost the only inhabitants of this immediate vicinity, but little life yet animated it. A few thieves and rag-pickers were returning to their rendezvous, and some hucksters, organ-grinders, and pea-nut sellers were emerging. A feeling of intense sadness shadowed her soul, as it had often done before, as she came forth into the narrow and filthy lane, and glanced at the wretched beings who were dodging into the alleys, or leaning sleepily from the windows, with besotted and

diseased countenances, and in listless rags.   Age, elsewhere venerable, and made kind and pious by the ordi-
nary chastisements of life, here wore only the sullen,
misanthropic scowl of those whose life is suffering
alone.   Womanhood, elsewhere the purifying element
of society, here gross, abandoned, and shameless,
teaches lisping infancy to swear like a pirate, instructs
the tongue to lie, and punishes the cheek if it blushes,
and persuades trembling honesty to pluck up courage
and steal.   Here infancy, even at the bosom of its
drunken mother, tastes a stimulant which starts it in
life with a besotting and ruinous thirst.   Here, out of
one generation loathsome with inherited and acquired
sins and diseases, is constantly issuing another, which,
by the law of hereditary transmission, enters the
world the involuntary heir of wicked hearts and diseased bodies, in which the soul of a saint could not
live righteously.   Here youth finds its school in the
tippling den, its college in the gambling hell, its
church in the brothel, and its home in the penitentiary
—wasting, in its continuous shifting between these
institutions so kindly fostered by most governments,
out of polite deference for the devil's love of liberty,
the small residue of health which inherited disease and
imbecility have left them.   Here maidenhood, elsewhere flowering in such moral and physical loveliness,
that poetry and prose have soared above all other fields

in the effort to embody it, and have soared in vain—maidenhood so purifying, so refining, so angelic when in virtue—

> " Standing with reluctant feet,
> Where the brook and river meet,
> Womanhood and childhood sweet,"

here plays a kindred part with whisky in the drama of ruin.

" Alas," thought Sister Clara, " what can be the effect of the death of Jesus of Nazareth, of whom they know little and care less, upon these people !   As well, I am convinced, might we look for a saving power in the cup of Socrates.   And yet, is it credible that God has created any portion of humanity to be from birth eternally beyond the moral possibility of salvation ? Can it be possible that that portion exists in the heart of a great and Christian city !   Oh," murmured the benevolent Sister, as the tears dimmed her eyes, " that I had a thousand lives, that I might give them all up to save these miserable wretches."   But what could she do, single-handed and alone !   As well attempt to mow down forests with a sickle.   She was without influence in the church, being controlled and not controlling, even in the limited sphere of her own daily labors.   Besides, the reply which she had ever received from the church, was that the souls of these people were as secure as any, and even more.   For nearly all

of them were unquestioning believers in the true
church, and thus better off than many whose smatter-
ing education and misdirected information led them
into heinous errors of doctrine, much more flagrant
than any acts of mere weakness and passion, and which
inevitably effected their endless damnation. There
were many of these who, almost in proportion to their
apparent darkness, were steadfastly attached to the
faith, received before their death full absolution for
their past sins, and as Paul brought the energy acquired in persecuting the church, when converted, into
the service of the church, so these wretches saved
money enough, even from the proceeds of their wickedness, to pay penance, and redeem their souls from
purgatory, and were saved, in overwhelming proof of
the great mercy of God, while thousands of the most
learned, upright, and well-meaning men, who were,
unfortunately, the most likely to be mistaken heretics,
did not repent, paid no penance, received no absolution,
and were irrevocably and endlessly damned in a lake
of fire and brimstone, in proof of his justice.

Of these facts there could be no doubt, as nearly
the whole Christian world, Catholic as well as Protestant, were united upon the point that belief in a particular creed was the only and necessary condition
precedent to salvation, the only question being as to
what the right creed might be. Upon this point the

argument was equally plain in favor of the truth of the Roman Catholic Church, and hence of the beneficent condition and final endless bliss of these seemingly wretched creatures, for it is evident that a just and benevolent God never would give the light to a few, and leave the great majority in darkness, when their eternal condition depended upon it. But, inasmuch as the Roman Catholic Church embraced nearly all of Christendom, and the small remnant of Protestants was divided into hundreds of disputing sects, each one of which differed within itself, so that probably there were scarcely two Protestants fully agreed upon all points, it follows that if salvation depends upon belief, the question will be whether one Protestant is to be saved, and the millions of the Roman Catholic Church are to be damned, or whether a benevolent God has so framed the truth that a majority of his people will believe it and be saved.

Revolving these thoughts not very satisfactorily in her mind, as she had often done with equal ill-success before, Sister Clara hurried quickly out of the dingy and loathsome district, and was threading her way homeward into more respectable thoroughfares and through increasing numbers of people, when she found herself suddenly environed by a crowd who seemed called together and excited by no usual circumstance. Lifting her eyes from the ground, where they had

been meditatively resting, they fell upon an object
which could not fail to enlist her sympathies. In the
midst of a great concourse of people, drawn together
apparently by absorbing curiosity, and followed by a
score of armed men, dressed partially in the uniform
of soldiers and of police, walked four persons, bearing
upon a litter which rested upon their shoulders, the
form of a young man.

He was wounded, for his arm was bandaged, and
bandages were around his waist, all red and oozing
with gore. Notwithstanding his wounds, his hands
were tied behind him, and his ancles bound as those
of a criminal. Beautiful locks of raven hair, parted
in mid forehead, fell gracefully down to his shoulders,
past features intellectual and handsome ; but now, as
he turned from side to side, and looked vacantly in
confused and dreamy wonder upon the crowd that were
bearing him on, that face was pale and full of anguish.

No inquiry was necessary to explain the scene before
her ; for from mouth to mouth the explanation was
passing—

" It is Conrad, the great pirate—Lafitte's lieutenant."

" They'll make short work of him," remarked a
burly merchant, standing upon his door-steps, to his
neighboring knight of the tape and scissors.

"That they will! And they ought to, for he is the veriest scoundrel unhung."

"I wonder if they will stop to try him? It seems like a waste of money to do so, when the proof is so plain. They caught him upon his return from some nefarious expedition, and shot him in the midst of his own crew. What better evidence do they want than that?"

"Sure enough! They say that the expedition of the pirates was to kidnap the heiress of a rich planter up the river, named Preston—a tall prize that. The old fellow owns a thousand niggers. She'd a' brought a nice ransom if they could have got her to Havana. But it seems the honest, unsuspecting old gentleman discovered something wrong after awhile, and set the police at work just in time to capture this fellow, though not to save his daughter, whom they succeeded in getting off with."

"Horrible—damnable! Just think what will become of the poor girl! The whole city ought to rise, as one man, and capture those bloody hounds. It serves us right. It has been rumored that for years this Conrad has passed, under a thin disguise, through the best society of New Orleans, and that some even knew him, and were bought off by a few niggers. I hope this Preston, who is more than half suspected, though nobody knows why, of being no better than he

ought to be, was one of those who took such a snake
to their hands. He ought to be bit, if only for appearing so crawling and mean as he does, if he is
honest, which I don't believe he is.".

Don't judge too harshly. I have seen many people
in my day, and I watched very carefully the face of
that young man as he passed just now, and what's
more, I was in the boat that picked him up and brought
him to shore, and manacled him, and I don't wonder
a country planter should be deceived by him."

"He had such a pious expression of overwhelmed
innocence," said another, "that in spite of the evidence
of my own eyes, for I saw him shot, every time I
looked at him I believed him innocent."

"Possible—what an incarnate devil !"

"You wouldn't say so after seeing him."

"What does he say for himself ?"

"Oh, most of the time, till they put the irons on
him, he was insensible ; and then he picked up, and
grew flighty, and acted off raving, about the girl and
about his mother, with a naturalness that would have
made your heart break."

"Gave the world some new lessons in fancy swear-
ing, I suppose," suggested the Scissors.

"Too cunning for that," replied the merchant—
"never dropped a word that a lady would not have
felt like loving him for—prayed that the spirit of his

motherwould be with him in his affliction, and prayed—
actually prayed, with his hands clasped in front of
him, and with tears streaming from his eyes—that
God would save 'Julia'—that's the girl he's kid-
napped, I suppose—from her terrible destiny. So he
did until we all felt shocked at the wretch, and tied
his hands behind him, to prevent him from going
through his blasphemous performances. Oh, he's the
devil's own."

"What a bird! Does he mean to make any one
believe he is innocent?"

"Not exactly, I shouldn't think; for when we
asked him if he was one of the pirates, and whether
he did not command at least the boat we saw him in—
for we saw him acting in command of it—and whether
he was not Conrad, he said, 'It's no use; you know
where you have found me.' And once, while he was
still insensible, one of us asked him his name, and he
unguardedly said, 'Defoe,' which, they say, is Conrad's surname."

"That is proof positive," rejoined Scissors, with the
dignity of a member of the Inner Temple.

"Proof! there couldn't be more proof. Yet, mark
my words—I'm in favor of hanging the man now;
and I believe the city would have seen it done instantly, if old Jackson, who is prophet, priest, and
king here now, hadn't got an inkling of it, and sent

the man to jail, under an escort, saying that he should have a trial ; for my opinion is that if that man is tried before a jury who can look at him, they'll admit his pious face in evidence, and let him go."

" We might as well be under martial law, and done with it, as to yield to that man's dictation in everything.   If I was the Governor I wouldn't stand it."

" The Governor don't like him, but dare not resist him for that very reason," said the merchant. " He is afraid of losing the little power he has got ; and my opinion in relation to that matter is, that if the British do come here, which nobody seems to have the slightest expectation of but old Jackson, then the Governor will settle down into private life, like an oyster into the mud."

"If I were the Governor of Louisiana, I wouldn't be so cowed by the irony old Tennessean, if he did know a little more than I did."

" Nor I."

" Why can't he stop to convince people, and not do just as he d—— pleases with everybody until everything is over, and then ask them if they see any objections to his policy ?"

"I tell you if the British ever do come here, we shall have such a kind of martial law as will make us all run over to them, for fear of General Jackson. Mark my words !"

Sister Clara had watched thus long the receding procession, for such it was, as if hesitating in her course ; and then, dashing quickly down by a nearer cross street, arrived before the procession at the city jail. The keeper received her kindly, for she was not an unfrequent visitor there, and promised her that, if possible, he would get permission for her to visit the coming prisoner as soon as the surgeon had dressed his wounds. The keeper left to obtain this permission, while she, not to lose her time, allowed the key of the outer door of the apartment of cells to be turned upon her, and wandering from door to door, talked kindly and familiarly with the inmates, occasionally dispensing little presents from her cornucopian basket.

CHAPTER XVIII.

IN PRISON.

"The quality of mercy is not strained,
But droppeth as the gentle dew from heaven
Upon the place beneath."—SHAKSPEARE.

Two hours had passed. The crowd of spectators, drawn thither by eager curiosity, had dispersed from around the jail. The physician had departed, and the Sister of Charity, full of the spirit of her vocation, had entered alone, and was bending tenderly over the wounded man. Few would have been allowed the privilege of being thus servicable to the wretched one, lest he might procure some means of self-destruction, but her name was a passport into the cell of the most abandoned, as it was a welcome at the threshold of poverty. Upon a hard pallet of boards, covered over with a blanket, reaching the length of the cell, yet still hardly long enough for him to recline at full length—the prisoner lay. The cell was about five feet wide, and its ceiling so low that many could not have stood erect under it. It was lighted only from the passage way through the iron bars of the door or gate, at which she entered, and which was now closed and locked upon her while the jailor waited and guarded without. Except this gate or door, the remaining sides of the room as well as the ceiling and floor, were dark and of solid masonry.

Sitting down upon the side of the hard pallet, upon which the prisoner lay, in alternate states of slumber, dreaming, raving and insensibility, she tenderly examined his wounds. The left arm was badly shattered, but the ball had passed it, entering his side, near the heart, and leaving a dangerous, and it was feared, a fatal wound. After ascertaining that the wounds had been dressed with a professional rudeness and skill equal to that with which they had been inflicted, she procured a pillow to be placed under his head, and another upon which to rest his wounded arm, which much relieved him.

When his lips moved, too, she bent over eagerly to catch their faintest mutterings. They were of a name that was familiar to her soul, and she heard it uttered at first with a shrinking feeling as of repugnance and horror.

"God forbid that Julia should ever mention thy name with the same unholy love," she murmured, bending still closer over his features, and fixing upon them an earnest and sorrowful glance.

Suddenly, as if reading more there than she could

solve, she lifted his head gently from its pillow and brought it more fully into the light which feebly entered at the door. For a moment her gaze was riveted upon it with eager intensity. Almost with rude suddenness she dashed back those beautiful waving locks of jetty black from his high manly brows.

Freshened by the water into which she had been bathing his brows, and disturbed and partially awakened from his slumber by the motion, he muttered the first coherent sentence—

"I am not he. Oh, God! I am innocent."

Sister Clara turned away for a moment, and shaded her brows with her hand, as if trying to recall some long lost, almost forgotten face or form. Then she fixed her riveted glance once again upon him with a still closer scrutiny and a still increasing intensity. And now, slowly and with eyes upturned to heaven, she lays his head back in its former position, murmuring—

"No—thou art not Conrad! Here is some fearful, some terrible error. My lovely son, thou art wholly innocent," she cried, now bathing his hand in her tears, and kissing it with a mother's affection. "This fair countenance is not the abode of wickedness. Thou art very like—but, thank God, thou art not he."

Then kneeling down by the bed-side, she clasped her hands and wept with emotion. For a moment she knelt with hands thus clasped, and eyes uplifted and streaming, as if in a fervent prayer of gratitude— then once more lifting up his head, and bringing his features into the light, she smiled as affectionately as a mother when looking at her first-born, and again turning back his silken locks, she kissed his brow, and restored his head to his pillow, and adjusted his limbs so that he might rest easily. She then rose and took up her little basket and knocked at the door of the cell. It was opened, and in a moment more Sister Clara had crossed the threshold, where so little of good and so much of evil crossed, and stood in the street.

CHAPTER XIX.

SANDY, THE VICTIM OF AN UNFORTUNATE ATTACHMENT.

She had not proceeded far when a voice behind her arrested her attention, and she turned around.

"What, is this you, Sandy ?"

"Yes 'em—Missa Clara," replied that worthy individual. "I've diskibbered her fust at last."

"You've found——"

"Miss Annette," replied the slave, grinning with evident inward elation. "I been seen her—my own eyes—last night, an' if you come along o' me, I den show you jis war she be, Missa Clara."

"This is good news if you are sure of its truth," exclaimed Sister Clara. "I will follow you, Sandy."

The slave darted off at a rapid and buoyant pace, evidently stimulated in his task by his infinite enjoyment at the approaching achievement of some long pending and important task, and turning occasionally to await the more staid and leisurely pace of Sister Clara.

In a few minutes they stood at the quay, where Sandy had appeared on the evening before, as we have seen, with his forgotten message. Here a scrutiny seemed necessary, for the prospect did not wholly realize Sandy's expectations.   Something had changed. He looked back at his route—it was the same.

· "Missa Clara, I certain shure I been come right, but she no here !"

" Who is not here ?"

" Ebberyting else de same—but de ship—I come here de berry last night—late, and I berry skered—I tell de capin Massa Defoe want to see him, an' I take de capin down to Massa Defoe. And dar was de capin in de ship, and dar wi' de capin, Miss Annette, an' I tink she looked at him berry kind and good. Ah ! say I, Miss Annette is de capin's wife. But now—no ship—no. capin—no Miss Annette—no nuffin'."

" Are you looking for the vessel ?" asked a portly man, in half uniform, who had been watching them with some attention, since they had stopped.

" Yes, massa. Tank you !" replied Sandy. " You know war she gone ?"

" Do you remember the name ?" asked the gentleman.

" De Flyin' Scud," answered Sandy.

· " And the captain?"

" Mass' Conrad "

"Did you go aboard of that vessel?" continued the stranger.

"Yeth, Massa—No—not 'zackly," said Sandy, timidly.

"Come along with me," said the stranger, advancing to him. "I'll show her to you. I thought you were not all right."

In another moment, and before the astonished Sandy was aware of his intentions, his hands were seized. The handcuffs snapped upon his wrists, and yelling wildly in his terror and flight, he was hurried swiftly away. The sympathizing Sister Clara heard the cries of the simple African.

"Wat dis for? De Lord help us. Sandy done nuffin'. De Lord help us. Wat Sandy stole? Oh, Lord!"

Unable at present to avert the catastrophe which had overtaken the poor negro, though she partly understood its nature, she retraced her steps towards the home of the Sisters of Charity.

CHAPTER XX.

THE TIME IS UP.

" Thou wealth to many poor, disgrace to many noble,
  Thou hope and fear, thou weal and woe, thou remedy, thou ruin,
  How thickly swarms of thought are clustering round To-morrow."
                                        PROVERBIAL PHILOSOPHY.

HAVING succeeded, as he supposed, in immuring his former accomplice and would-be betrayer, Conrad Defoe, within the walls of a dungeon, awaiting with dread certainty a felon's doom, Mr. Preston returned to his accustomed hotel.

His mind was restless and ill at ease. Whatever might have been his feelings in sacrificing Julia to the exigencies of his pecuniary embarrassments, he was not prepared for the turn in the wheel of fortune which had consigned his daughter Ada to the fate intended for another, and thus stripped him at once of every kindred tie.

Not that his wounded affections, as a father, caused him very great pain, but the prospect of the utter loss of caste in society, which inevitably ensues to the base

when poverty comes upon them, coupled with the possibility of arraignment, exposure, and condign punish-
ment for the criminal relation in which he had stood
towards Conrad and his fellows, filled him with apprehension.

In this state of mind, as soon as the clock had
struck ten, he left his apartments at the hotel, and
passing into —— Street, entered a building once occupied as a gentleman's residence, whose ancient architectural frippery was now smeared over with the tin
signs of a nest of attorneys, looking like a last year's
bird's nest filled with spiders.

Passing up several of the flights of stairs and along
a narrow passage-way, as if diving into this recess for
one of the poorest or meanest of the fraternity, he
stopped at length before a door upon which was a
small "tin shingle" bearing the name " Snacks !"

He opened the door and entered.   A very lank person, in a seedy black coat, whose skirt hung from his armpits to his knees, with legs like two stilts, whose cadaverous appearance was heightened by close-fitting knee-
breeches of faded velvet, terminating in a substantial
pair of blue woolen stockings, which in turn were buried
in a long pair of slab-soled cowhide shoes, turned slowly
round, and with a silent nod indicated to Mr. Preston
to take a chair.

Everything about this man was so long that it was

tedious to follow it to its legitimate conclusion. His gaunt, skeleton fingers coiled around Mr. Preston's hand like the grasp of five anacondas. His forehead, nose and chin rivalled each other in longitude, though his chin bore off the palm. Long files of papers lay by his side. A very long brief in a tall, slim hand-writing, of some exceedingly protracted case, was in his hand, which, however, he laid aside as Mr. Preston sat down.

Then turning to the latter, he wreathed the wrinkles upon his long face into a peculiar labyrinthian smile, and drawled as if his organs of speech, like an unruly legislature, no sooner commence business, than they endeavor to adjourn *sine die*—

" Glad—to—see—you,—Mr.—Preston. I—'spose —you—come—to—pay—"

" No, Mr. Snacks, I am sorry to say I am not prepared to pay the ten thousand francs to-day."

" N—o—t !" drawled Snacks.

" No, Mr. Snacks. I have done my utmost, but the plan by which I hoped to raise the money has utterly failed. I will promise, however, in a few months, if you will grant me that time, to satisfy your debt by another means which is sure of success."

Mr. Snacks had occupied the time during which Mr. Preston had uttered this speech in a long sigh,

Then he turned slowly around, and running his long fingers over a list of court-terms pasted upon the door of his book-case, he said—

"Yes,—I—can !"

"You can give me the time then ?" inquired Mr. Preston. "Mr. Snacks, you are my friend ; sir, I know you are. I admire your generosity, and, sir, I shall reward it. To the extent of my means, sir, you shall be rewarded ! I understand you rightly, sir, that you can give me the time," said he, startled at the expression of ineffable surprise with which Mr. Snacks' eye slowly weathered around towards him, and the altitude to which the legal functionary's brows were climbing as he looked at him.

"No," drawled Mr. Snacks, "never—extend—but twice. Am—very—glad—I have a—chance—to—serve—you,—but—sorry—I—can't—embrace—it. I must—fore—close !"

"When ?"

"As—soon—as—I—can."

"When will that be ?"

"Next—term."

"And when will that be ?"

"On—the—return—of the—chancellor."

"Will you be good enough, Mr. Snacks, to tell me when that will be ?" said Preston impatiently.

"To—mor—row !"

"Do you mean to say that you can and will seize upon my whole real and personal estate, and make a beggar of me to-morrow?"

At the word "say," Mr. Snacks commenced at the same imperturbable pace to repeat—

"To—mor—row!"

"Is there no alternative? Good God, do not ruin me!" exclaimed Preston with emotion and terror. "Mr. Snacks, I appeal to you as a man, as a Christian, I beg your pardon, sir, as a Jew, what time, if it be only a few weeks, will you give me to raise this sum?"

"To—mor—row."

In that look Mr. Preston read his destiny. In those words he heard and felt his doom. A film came over his eyes, and he thought he would have sunk upon the seat from which he had risen.

How, he knew not, for he saw and thought of nothing on the way, he returned to his hotel apartments. A vision of horrors rose before him. Floods of grief, rage, remorse and chagrin poured in upon his soul, and he rushed out of the hotel, as he had often done before, to seek relief at the source of his misfortunes and the cause of his crimes—the faro table. Just as he reached the street, a messenger informed him that the mother superior of the mother house of the Sisters of Mercy, was desirous to see him. Wondering what could be the reason of a call for his presence from such a source, he changed his course and hastened to the house indicated.

The streets were filled with the munitions and array of war, and the preparations of the arbitrary Tennessee captain, for the approaching contest with the veterans who had fought under Wellington on the Peninsula.

CHAPTER XXI.

PHILOSOPHY.

Hamlet.—" There are more things in heaven and earth, Horatio,
       Than are dreamed of in your philosophy."—SHAKSPEARE.

EARLY one morning Ada arose, and looking out of her window, for the first time since her captivity, her eyes fell upon the joyful spectacle of land. True, from her window, the scene was rather desolate than inviting, for though the sun had hardly risen from the sea, which calm and bathed in his glory, seemed like a plain of molten fire—though the sea itself was so motionless, unrippled, and still, beautifully reflecting from its placid bosom the blue sky and sailing clouds, yet the land which met her view was but a continuous ledge of precipitous rocks, without entrance or harbor, stretching away as far as the eye could reach. The nearest rose apparently to the height of several hundred feet.

"Ah, how delightful !" exclaimed Annette, this moment rushing into the room. "Cheer up, my drooping prisoner—I have good news for you."

"What, pray ?" said Ada, starting.

"We are at the Festal Island—the fairy Island—

the bewitching, the entrancing island. Only look at it," she continued, joyfully, encircling Ada's waist in her pretty arm, and drawing her to the window.

"I see nothing but a long ledge of rocks," replied Ada, smiling, "which would be perfectly horrid were it not that I so long for a glimpse of land, that the dreariest prospect is welcome. I am sure there is not a green thing upon it."

"Oh, yes," said Annette.   "These cliffs hide nearly all of its beauty ; but look far away to the right," she said, pressing Ada's head through the cabin window, where she might see farther in that direction. "Do you not see the top of Magnolia Grove ?   What a rich, dark, tropical green it wears !   What an exuberance of foliage ! Oh, methinks I can almost scent," she said, delicately snuffing her little nose towards the island, "the rich fragrance which is wafted down by the morning breeze from the groves of oranges and fields of bananas and pineapples."

"You have been here before, then ?" inquired Ada. "Why have you never told me of this paradise of sweets ?"

"Oh, I thought it would be such a glad surprise !" exclaimed Annette, now popping her head from the window, and now waltzing and skipping around the room, and clapping her hands with the gaiety of a school girl on the first day of vacation, "and here I have been breaking the charm which I had so carefully reserved for you, by telling you all. Come, Miss, let us take one more look at Magnolia Grove," she said, thrusting her head out of the window, "and now let's pack up."

"Pack up! You do not mean that we are going ashore, Annette?" inquired Ada.

"Of course I do," replied Annette.

"And leave this hated vessel?" exclaimed Ada.

"I certainly do not think the vessel will accompany us very far inland," smiled Annette. "But why you should hate the innocent bit of live oak I cannot see—you who have, with the joys of conquest, cheated captivity of her sadness."

"Ah, no," sighed Ada—"under any other circumstances I would feel very happy in the love of Mr. Howard; and sometimes I do, as it is. But how can I help sighing very, very often? Oh, no, Annette; I fear I am doing fearfully wrong. I am unhappy—very, very un——"

"Do not speak thus sadly, dear," said Annette, embracing her tenderly. "Mr. Howard is in high spirits at the thought of being left for a short time at the island, and told me to assure you—for Lafitte and his officers were running up and down the companion-way, busily preparing for landing, so that he could not safely visit you—that this haunt of the pirates is a suspected one, in the very midst of the Florida keys, through which vessels of every nation are almost daily passing, and that our being here greatly increases the chances of our deliverance."

"Was ever a person so sanguine as Arthur?" smiled Ada. "Alas! I have not his hope nor your light heart. I look for no deliverance but in—death."

"Oh, Ada!" exclaimed Annette, almost weeping with emotion. "It is not kind to him, it is not true to yourself, to be so sad on this morning of joy ; dry your tears."

"Oh, Annette! our position is so terrible. How completely are we at the mercy of these wild outlaws. Sometimes I wonder that I, or you, or any other person should have been treated by them with such gentleness. But who knows at what moment all this may change, and we be made the victims of their brutal natures!" And the shrinking, trembling girl wept at the pictures which her imagination painted. "But tell me, why do we leave this vessel, where we have been unharmed, and what is to become of us?"

"And can it be that my fickle little bird is regretting to leave the cage in which she now feels so secure, to flit in freedom among the lime trees and make vocal the air of the magnolia groves of Festal Island ? But as you are so inquisitive as to demand for what reason our captors do with us as they will, I can only answer, because there are none here to prevent them from doing their pleasure. If you ask for their motive for removing us to the island, it is doubtless that in case of the capture of this vessel, not only may we be secure from recapture, which were comparatively a trifling loss, though it would prevent them from realizing the large ransom they expect from us, but they also would be secure from disclosure of this their great hiding place, a revelation which would immediately lead to their effectual overthrow, and which they have endeavored to avoid by directing the public attention as much as possible to Barrataria, where a few of their smuggling vessels, and but little piratical wealth, gives a semblance of comparative honesty to their business."

" Comparative honesty!" exclaimed Ada. " I have heard you express your admiration of their mode of life, and claim for them the merit of smiting the oppressor and succoring the oppressed. Pray, tell me whether you do really regard them as valiant knights-errant or as monsters of evil ?"

"Ah !" replied the ingenious Annette, " everything is good or evil, not intrinsically, but according to the point of view from which we look at it, and that point always happens to be self. There is no vice, no crime, which seen from some point of view and placed in contrast with something worse, cannot be justified and shown to be good, while on the other hand, seen from another point of view, and contrasted with something better, it can, with equal clearness, be proved to be evil. All depend upon the stand-point from which we look at it, and as that stand-point is ourselves, all things come to us like strange dogs by whatever name we choose to call them. One will call such and such things 'good,' and show how the title fits them. To him they are good, and he worships them as an Egyptian worships his cow. Another will call them 'evil,' and they answer to the name just as well. The Christian lifts his hands in holy horror at all human action, and says 'it is impossible that the human heart shall conceive of any good thought,' and consequently that whatever we do is wrong. This brings no charge against the pirate, for in doing wrong to the utmost of his power continually, he does no differently from all others, and to ask him to do a good thing is to ask an impossibility. Not to do what it is impossible for him to do is certainly no moral wrong, and therefore whatever he does is right. Religion is philosophy enveloped in a thin veil of absurdity. Remove the absurdity, and the naked philosophy appears, saying, 'Whatever is, is right.' When thus both religion and philosophy acquit wickedness, what shall poor Annette say ?"

"Poor Annette should listen to the teachings of her

own heart," replied Ada, "and not trust to such blinding sophistry."

" But, alas, my poor weak heart teaches me only to distrust its own teachings," replied Annette.

"Oh, Annette, Annette," replied Ada weeping, " your mind is stronger than mine, and I can scarcely believe it has had no other advantages than those you tell me ; but do not, for pity's sake, lead me into such dark places. Do not take away my star of faith, faintly as it now shines through the cloud of my transgressions, and leave me only the dull lamp of my reason. There was a time when I could have directed you to a higher authority, but, alas, I fear—" Ada with downcast eyes stood trembling and silent.

The jingle of a bell now summoned Annette to the cabin of Lafitte, and she vanished, but returned in a moment, and entered in a glad, frisking, hop-skip-and-jump style, which contrasted singularly with her recent gravely philosophical mood, upon the all-absorbing business of " packing up."

In two hours this task had been accomplished, and Ada, permitted by her swarthy jailors to lean upon the arm of Mr. Howard, was conducted with Annette through the narrow passage-way, which she had not before crossed since her imprisonment, and up the companion-way to the deck. Once more the blue heavens, enlivened with their fleecy clouds, hung over her head. It was cheerful to emerge again into the open day, and breathe the fresh, free air of heaven ; but it was terrible to meet also the glances of the crowd of silent, ill-looking outlaws who thronged the deck, and filled the yawl into which they were requested to descend. Ada's joy shrunk into fear. In a moment they were swiftly gliding over the long deep swells towards the wild, mysterious, and forbidding battlements of rock, which Ada scanned earnestly, but in vain, for some crevice or place of entrance.

CHAPTER XXII.

FESTAL ISLAND.

> " To sit on rocks, to muse o'er flood and fell,
>   To slowly trace the forest's shady scene,
>   Where things that own not man's dominion dwell,
>   And mortal foot hath ne'er or rarely been ;
>   To climb the trackless mountain all unseen,
>   With the wild flock that never needs a fold,
>   Alone o'er steeps and foaming falls to lean—
>   This is not solitude : 'tis but to hold
> Converse with nature's charms, and view her stores unrolled."
>
> BYRON.

As they drew near to the precipitous rocks, they seemed to present no less smooth, even, and unbroken a barrier. Not a break, chink, or crevice relieved the monotonous majesty of this dissevered mountain, which thus presented its section to the waves which beat, and foamed, and surged around its feet in frothy impotence. Still the boat swiftly darted towards the impassable barrier as hopefully as it would to its chosen harbor. Suddenly, as Ada was about bracing herself for the shock, for it seemed as if the boat were driving with all its speed against the very base of the solid cliff, a curtain of canvas, painted in nice imitation of the rock, parted, and the boat glided smoothly through into a vaulted tunnel or cave, the entrance of which was barely broad and high enough to admit the yawl, but which soon enlarged into a vaulted chamber, where the echoes returned to each stroke of their oars in the placid waters, alone indicated the great size of the cavern, for all was darker than the blackest midnight known to dwellers upon the surface.

Resting their oars, the boatswain applied a match to his lantern, and in another moment its imperfect light had kindled the cavern of darkness into a palace of beauty.   The distant, irregular ceiling glistened as if studded with myriad gems of every hue and lustre, or as if the stars of heaven, enamored with Neptune, had fled from the day into this festal hall of his, that he might woo them.

As their oars rippled the placid waters, a bright phosphoric light shone from them ; while here and there the sides of the cavern exposed dark entrances into other rooms, the farther sides of which glistened more dimly under the fainter light which reached them.

"How lovely !" exclaimed Ada, as the boat shot silently and swiftly into other chambers, some of them even larger than the first—some of them mere passage ways, beneath which they stooped to pass through.

At length they came to one which, as they entered,

presented no other apparent opening than that through which they had come, and again, as the boat seemed about to strike the solid rock of the cavern, the obstacle before it parted like a curtain, and they emerged into the open day, in the midst of a calm crystal lagoon, around the sides of which the unrivaled richness of tropical vegetation, flourishing in undisturbed luxuriance and beauty, burst like a dream of Arcadia upon their mute, wondering gaze. This lagoon, of but a few hundred yards in width, soon narrowed, as they dashed over it, into a mere passage, very narrow and winding, with coral shores and bottom, through which they passed into one of much larger dimensions.

Nearly circular, stretching far away in either direction, ran the groves of magnolia, cocoa, and live oak, and here and there the palm tree, the pine of the tropics, towered in stately and graceful dignity. Within this wall of verdure the roar of the great ocean was unheard, and a beautiful little world slept there, effectually shut in from the great world around it.

Ada could not help surveying the fairy scene with pleasure and joy, that even the desolate and unknown places of the earth were thus filled with beauty, and prepared to delight the eye of man when he should come to occupy them.

Upon one side of this lagoon was the pirate settlement, consisting of half a dozen low, rudely constructed houses, surrounded by rude gardens. Drawn up on the shore, were many beautifully modelled and painted boats. Passing no nearer than was necessary to the "village," and through a similar narrow passage-way, they entered and crossed a third lagoon of similar appearance, though smaller, upon the opposite side of which they landed. So accustomed had Ada become to novelty of every kind, that she was not surprised to find two tough little Shetland ponies, whose manes and tails almost reached the ground, held by a mute negro boy, in waiting for them. So inviting did the long green grass of the shaded plain before them appear, that Ada would have preferred to walk, and almost envied the little pony the pleasure with which he trotted over his green carpet, had not the diminutive proportions and grace of the pony himself, made her long to sit once more in the saddle. Accepting, therefore, the direction of their guide, and of Annette, to whom the whole scene was familiar, the ladies mounted the two ponies and trotted leisurely into the wood, Mr. Howard walking by their side.

"Ah!" exclaimed Ada involuntarily, as her eyes wandered through the magnificent trunks, and up among the sweeping branches, which terminated far up in a firmament of foliage, through which faint crevices admitted the day, "methinks, when I look at those glimmering crevices in yonder foliage, I am reminded of the beautiful Indian conception, which teaches that the stars are eyelets in the crystal sphere of heaven, to let the glory of the outer world shine through upon the darkness of this !"

"I thought you would lapse into a poetical dream here, if anywhere in the wide, wide world !" said Annette smiling. "Ah ! long may it be ere my invading friends shall disturb me in the quiet enjoyment of this celestial retreat ; I ask no other home."

A short ride brought them to a clearing, or open space, in which rose a lightly constructed, but neatly finished cottage of two stories, the second surrounded by a verandah, and embowered in lime and orange trees. The air wafted from an adjacent thicket of pine-apples, came loaded with delightful odors, and all things seemed thrown around this snugly embowered and concealed retreat which might gratify the senses or delight the imagination. Nor did the exterior of the woodland cottage surpass the interior in appliances to the comfort and the taste. The rooms were tastefully, and even richly furnished, with levies upon the necessaries and luxuries of every clime. Music, books, and birds were ready to charm the soul with their varied harmonies.

CHAPTER XXIII.

A DREAM.

"I had a dream—it was not all a dream."—BYRON.

MANY days glided rapidly and happily by to the captives, if indeed their liberty to roam unrestrained over the island, could deserve the name of captivity Mute, black menials who, in response to Ada's inquiries, opened their mouths and revealed their mutilated tongues, silently supplied their every want, and attended to the cultivation of the small plantation attached to the house. Except these they saw no other person, for the pirate village was some two miles distant on the shore of the second lagoon.

Mr. Howard availed himself of these morning and evening rides on horseback over the island, to enjoy more abundantly and freely the society of the gentle Ada, while she daily yielded a happier and more absolute homage to her lover's passion. Indeed, even she began to realize that she was the captive not so much of the terrible Conrad and of Lafitte, as of the elegant and captivating Howard. It was his step, at which her pulses thrilled, her cheek flushed, and her heart beat. Her whole being responded to the tones of his soft voice, as the strings of the harp thrill under the touch of the skillful player, and constant, unintermitted communion, rapidly fanned the flame of passion in their souls. Hours, days, flew by uncounted, unregretted. Their bliss knew no bounds ; they were very, very happy. So wild and strange, so unlike her whole previous life had been her recent experience, that Ada began to live a dream life, and all that was real seemed to her as a doubtful dream, and in return her dreams often borrowed the vividness of reality. It was after the noon of a balmy and beautiful December day, in that clime where winter comes only like a gentle zephyr to fan the summer-heated brow to a delightful coolness ; Howard had for once consented to accompany Annette instead of Ada upon an afternoon ride, and Ada, throwing herself upon a couch, closed her eyes that she might visit for a few moments, in thought, old Lindenhall, with its tawny faces, its peaceful security, its delightful scenery, and especially might commune for a brief though mournful season with the spirit of her sister. From this revery she passed to sleep, and in that sleep she dreamed.

She saw two souls upon their downward flight from heaven. They were clothed in mist, and had the form of dew-drops. Side by side they descended and

had almost united in one. They were blending together, when in their fall the thorn of a rose divided
them, and they fell on opposite sides of the scented
bush, which bloomed on a tuft of earth, between two
springs, one of them clear, the other disturbed by an
evil spirit. One of the dew-drops, with its precious
burden, fell in one spring and the other in the other.
The fountains were not connected, but welled forth
far up in the mountains of the north-west, and it so
happened that their waters flowed down on the opposite sides of the mountain. And the distance between
the two souls, borne along on their respective currents,
was greater and greater every day forever, until the
one was lost in the great ocean of the west, and the
other in that of the east.

While the dreamer still gazed at the two oceans,
their appearance changed. Over that one into which
the waters of the turbid spring had flown, flew the
same evil spirit which had disturbed the spring, and
forthwith it became a billowy sea of human forms,
the waves of which were but-their heavings and fall-
ings as they writhed in intense agony. And she saw
one sparrow alight upon that ocean shore for a pebble.
It took one and fluttered away in the direction of a
distant star, from which the swift-winged light would
not reach the earth in sixty centuries ; and an
angel whispered that for milllluns of centuries the

little bird would flutter onwardto the distant star, and at last deposit its pebble and return for another. So should that sparrow repeat its flight until no pebbles should be left upon the sea-shore, and the prairies and the mountains be removed, nay, the whole earth should, pebble by pebble, have been borne to that distant planet, yet that writhing ocean of agony would remain the same.

On the other hand, for each drop of the ocean, supplied from the crystal spring, there was a resurrection of joyous life and bliss. Broader than the continents of earth, nay, from the earth to the stars, stretched out than the sea of angelic faces, with love in their eyes and harps in their hands. Every moment was one of rapture, like the first thrill of joy in the heart of the accepted lover or the forgiven penitent. The atmosphere they breathed, the rivers of life in which they bathed, the nector of wisdom they drank, the delicious manna of purity upon which they fed, the conversation which they indulged in with each other, the beauties of the world around them, which they learned, the hymns of adoration and worship which they sang, all were not merely pleasant, or even delightful, they were the food of an intensely blissful intoxication that never subsided. For when the little sparrow, in his long flights to the distant star, had removed the earth, their joy was still increasing.

Trembling with the emotions excited by this dream, Ada awoke and wept. Her eyes had not the quiet, serene light which was their wont. Her expression was one of anxious and timid unrest. She rose from her couch, and tried to kneel down by it, but without praying, she burst into tears, and threw herself once more upon the bed, murmuring—

"Oh! whither, whither have I drifted?" and went to sleep, and again she dreamed.

Surrounded by a countless host, she stood upon the brink of a precipice, before which yawned a deep, but not forbidding abyss; it was not forbidding, for it seemed a pleasant valley filled with inviting fruits, languishing forms, and happy sounds and scenes of fearless pleasure. A mist rose out of this abyss, through which she was faintly able to discern the spires and temples of a distant country, which her heart instinctively prompted her to try to gain. Angels flew backward and forward over this abyss at pleasure, but the only bridge by which wingless mortals might cross it, was a single hair suspended from side to side. Whosoever ventured upon the hair, depending upon his own skill to balance himself, fell; and though all below, as nearly as could be discerned through the rising mist, seemed indicative of pleasure only, such as fell invariably threw towards their friends who stood upon the precipice a last glance of unutterable anguish and woe. This alone informed them that the abyss, notwithstanding its appearance of gratification, was full of unhappiness and pain. But whosoever approached the abyss, and were sensible enough to perceive their own inability to cross it without aid from above, and besought that aid, such were upheld and steadied by angelic powers, which hovered around about them, and they walked, in fear and trembling, safely over, and were welcomed to the embrace of a shepherd.

Seeing this, Ada besought the heavenly powers to aid her, and ventured forth. But when she had gone a short way in safety, the beauty of the scenes in the vale beneath her, and her love for some whom she recognized there, drew her down, and she felt the hold of the angels loosening, and herself not unwillingly descending to other embraces, while her sister Julia, who had started just before her, with eyes turned upward in pleading faith and constancy, saw her not, but continued on to the farther shore. And now a quick, intermittent fever, of alternate bliss and pain, thrilled and consumed her. One minute her pulses bounded in ecstatic joy—the next her heart sickened with heaviness and woe. Her whole body also vibrated each moment between misery and delight, pain and pleasure. But swiftly as she fell deeper and deeper, the intervals of pleasure grew less frequent, more brief, and less ecstatic, until anon, the burnings of bodily pain, and of mental anguish and remorse, convulsed her frame. Flame, not blood, coursed through her veins. Every disease peculiar to the various parts of the human body attacked those parts, and mercilessly fed upon the deathless agony which they could not in mercy consume or kill. The beautiful vale around her, in which she had thought to sink as into a pleasant couch, resolved itself on a nearer view into a lake, not of water nor of fire, but of loathsome, leprous, corpse-like beings, in monstrous forms, half man and half beast and serpent, which rolled and writhed together in one commingled mass, swimming in the sweat of their agony. Their faces were now livid with fiendish rage—now black with choking anguish and despair. No hope, no love, no trust or confidence beamed in their downcast eyes. Nor amidst all this seething, rolling mass was there a single one struggling to look up or to rise; but each one was striving, with all his might, to bury himself beneath his fellows, from the tearful glances of the angels who flew over the abyss, and vainly offered to assist them to rise from their lost condition.

Incessant wailings rent the air, and formed the horrible music of the fiery vale.

Into this damned sea of suffering humanity, with all its pains and terrors, Ada felt herself sinking. She shrieked. The spires and temples of the distant city were growing dim to her vision. The infernal tortures, seizing upon every vital part, racked her. Each nerve which was capable of sensation endured its separate agony, increasing with every moment. -

The miseries of insanity, without its forgetfulness, made cruel sport of her imagination, and in each chamber of her soul a separate devil laughed in delirious misery. A dream within this dream increased its horrors by a clear vision of the purity, beatitude, and holy bliss of heaven, where harmonious spirits listened to the music of the spheres, and learned new lessons daily of the wonders of the universe, whose minds swept all time, conceived all beauty, comprehended all wisdom ; whose hearts were steeped in love and intoxicated with bliss, whose every nerve thrilled with delight, and whose hymns were the ceaseless carols of overflowing joy.

The dreamer could no longer endure the vision— with a shriek and a moan she awoke, weeping bitterly.

"What is the matter?" asked Annette, who had returned, and had been bending over her during the convulsions with which the dream had been accompanied, "you have had a sad dream."

"Ah, Annette, Annette, reason with me no more," she cried, "that there is no contrast between good and evil."

For days after her wild, delirious dream, Ada was

exceedingly sad. No efforts of Mr. Howard or Annette could avail aught to enliven her. Her cheek grew pale, her form thin. The accustomed ride no longer conferred its usual pleasure. She was deaf to the songs of birds, blind to the loveliness of flowers, indifferent utterly to all things. Her soul seemed fast settling into the deepest despondency. Her interviews with Mr. Howard began and ended not in smiles, but in tears. From what reason she knew not, but this had not continued many days before Mr. Howard, Annette and Ada were again required to embark on board the " Flying Scud." Mr. Howard kindly expressed a hope that the change of air might be found a providential interposition to restore her sinking health and spirits.

CHAPTER XXIV.

THE VEIL REMOVED.

" With her hands clasp'd, her lips apart and pale,
The maid had stood, gazing upon the veil
From which these words, like south winds through a fence
Of Kerzrah flowers, came filled with pestilence;
So boldly uttered too! as if all dread
Of frowns from her, of virtuous frowns, were fled,
And the wretch felt assured that, once plunged in,
Her woman's soul would know no pause in sin."

MOORE.

As one experience after another revealed more fully to the gentle and intellectual Julia the character of the refuge to which she had flown, she found at first much to displease, and gradually sufficient to disgust, if not to terrify her. Instead of inviting the mind to periods of holy thought and study, the rules of the institution and the efforts of its members seemed to commit the real sin of punishing imaginary transgressions by unnecessary pains. Instead of contemplation, which should purify and invigorate the soul, self-mortifications, in an unexpected manner and absurd degree, were inflicted to weaken and abuse the body. The beauty of humility she deeply appreciated, but she had none of that pride which, pluming itself upon its own humbleness, could bear up and stimulate her refined and educated soul to plod constantly and unnecessarily through a routine of menial drudgery, for which neither her education nor her physical strength at all qualified her. No sister cared less than she for the bauble of dress or ornament; but she had too much good sense to suppose that it was any worse to fritter away our minds in cultivating ornament, than equally to fritter them away in avoiding all that was seemly, or that piety was assisted by unnecessarily wearing garments as uncomfortable to the body as they were unsightly to the eye.

For delicate food she cared not, but a coarse, vulgar diet, which immediately affected her health and spirits, and rendered her less fit to perform any of the arduous menial, and not less arduous devotional duties assigned to her, was not at all to her taste. Far was her natural disposition from being otherwise than submissive to the direction and counsel of her superiors, or amiably pliant to the wishes of those whose wishes were the more joyfully obeyed because uttered as requests. But nothing can be more painful to the truly sensitive and refined mind, than to be subjected to the accidental authority of our inferiors in mind and heart, who, conscious of an inferiority in those respects, endeavor to compensate for it by additional exercise of those faculties in which they excel, *viz.*, insolence and rudeness.   Of the delightful pleasures of parental and filial affection, Julia had, it is true, possessed little experience, but her union to Ada had taught her that there are earthly affections which approach very near to the intensity of angelic loves, and such affections of a real sister contrasted strongly with the cold maxims with which her self-styled sisters excused themselves from taking any interest in each other or in her, by fixing their eyes on their work, and their thoughts on heaven.   "If ye love not those whom ye have seen, how shall ye love Him whom ye have not seen ?" she said to herself.   And again, when she became more fully aware of the sufferings, both voluntary and involuntary, which the sisters endured, and when she detected the consequences of thus abusing themselves, and throwing back the precious boons of life and health in the very teeth of the Giver, in the wan cheek, the hectic flush, the fragile form, and the hollow cough of those around her, and when she reflected how much of this martyrdom of the body was self-inflicted and unnecessary, and how it tended to sin by causing a corresponding gloominess and moroseness among the sisters, and how little of it ever went forth to work a change over the face of a sin-stricken world ; in a word, when she slowly began to realize how much of energy and pious zeal was immured within those and other convent walls to molder and waste in inaction—the effect of the pealing organ, and the solemn, impressive chaunt, and the imposing beauty of the ceremonies of the church died away, and often she felt as if her life had displayed more true and practical benevolence when relieving the ills of her father's small plantation world, than when exorcised by the severe discipline of a Sister of Charity. This was to her a sore disappointment, for she had thought in becoming a sister to be an humble instrument in the hands of God of relieving the distresses of mankind. Instead of which she felt that she, and most of her sisters, were cut off from those distresses, and from all except that self-manufactured misery which was the consequence of their penances, fastings, and labors. In short, when she reflected upon the usefulness they might have wrought in the limited but potent sphere of domestic influence, as daughters, sisters, wives and mothers, it seemed doubtful to her whether they were not adding to, rather than diminishing the sum total of human suffering.

While revolving these thoughts, so opposite to the dreams with which she entered the institution, in her mind, the time at last arrived when, by the consent of the Mother Superior, she was permitted the long-sought boon of seeing, for the first time since the hours of forgotten infancy—her mother.

That interview, while it exalted her appreciation of the amiable virtues of Sister Clara, and thereby redeemed the clouded picture of convent life, of which she saw in Sister Clara so fair and lovely an embodiment, yet renewed in her heart the strongest of all ties which could bind her to the outer world, and which she had thought, and even hoped, was forever severed.

The assurances given her by Sister Clara, seemed to drive away from her soul the monster of wickedness which haunted it, and to restore to her arms the pure, the exalted, the noble Walter Defoe, whom, with the slightest food for faith, she again loved with subdued, but passionate ardor. How ready was she to believe—how joyfully she felt assured that the cloud which rested over him was one of mystery and unfortunate coincidence, but not of guilt ; and if not of guilt, was she not called upon—by all that was true, and devoted, and holy in the deepest and most soul-thrilling of all the affections—to fly to him, to share with him his shame and imprisonment, as willingly as she would have shared his fortunes or his liberty ? How poorly was she fulfilling the Christian mission of love, when immured in a cold receptacle of frozen and chilled human hearts, and occupied wholly by servile and menial labors, but a tithe of which seemed to go to fill the urn of charity, while he whom God, by the strongest affection of which we are capable, had bound indissolubly to her, was pining upon the bed of pain, wounded—suffering—perhaps dying, without one kind friend to alleviate his miseries, or offer up a prayer for his departing soul. Agitated by a conflict of various emotions, and unable clearly to perceive her duty, she was glad to flee for refuge to the soothing relief of the confessional. There she had been wont, and especially of late, to unburden all her soul—to open the volume of her sinful and erring thoughts in the presence of the holy representative of God. Why should she not freely do so now, when the most important of all the questions which she should be called upon in this life to decide, and in the future to account for, must soon be decided, and that, too, forever !

As she entered the cell, she met a young and pretty Sister, who looked younger and prettier under the influence of an ill-concealed smile and blush, which seemed to Julia little in keeping with the sacredness of the task she had just fulfilled. She thought little of it, however, for since her entrance within the holy walls, she had often painfully witnessed the degree to which frequent and stated repetitions of prescribed devotional exercises lessen the reverence of the devotee, and convert his worship into a trifling and heartless mummery. Lamenting this thought, the door of the cell closed upon her, and she approached and kissed the ground before the worthy father. Raising her eyes from thence, she saw in him not the reverend and aged priest, Father Reilly, to whom she had previously confessed, but a young and dark man, whose lustrous eye and soft, youthful form ill accorded with the gloomy habit in which he was shrouded.

Hesitating for a moment whether to unfold the story of her heart to him in whom, spite of his habit, her imagination found it so difficult to recognize a spiritual father, she in a few moments, with eyes modestly fixed upon the ground, and unmindful of the effect of her presence or her story upon the young father, found herself revealing the inmost thoughts of her guileless bosom—even the touching story of her love. As if conscious that a person of his habits of contemplation and heavenly meditation could know nothing of the intensity of such a passion, or of the power it possesses to swerve us from duty, and distort even our notions of duty itself, the gentle Julia pathetically, and with unconscious eloquence, described its thrilling power, until a glow of earthly admiration spread over the face of the young priest.

"I can see but two ways by which you may escape the suffering inflicted upon your soul in consequence of this guilty passion," he remarked at length.

"And what are they, holy father?"

The first—to yield to it, which would be to return

to the malevolent and bitter world which you have left, which, having once walked in the better path, you should pray earnestly that you may never do."

"And the other?"

"Is to remain here, and seek to mitigate the power of this guilty love, by directing it to other objects, or replacing it by holier affections."

"But, reverend father, I could love no other; and even if I could, would it not be a fresh sin? Besides, I see no one but the sisters and the priests. Whom could I love?"

"Whether you could love no other, my dear daughter," replied the priest, "I suppose it would be difficult for any one situated as you are to prophesy.— Whether it would be an additional sin if you should, it were well to leave to your confessor. But of this be assured—the daughter whose weakness must needs give the reins to her affections, is happier when those affections stray not beyond the pale of the church."

Already the atmosphere of sacredness and holiness, which had hitherto seemed to Julia to fill the chamber of confessional, vanished, and she felt a stifling sense of vacuity, as if a world of nothingness were concentrated in the being before her, or as if he were one of those dark absorbents, sucking good out of all around it, but radiating no spiritual light in return.

From the desire more fully to be assured of this,

to her, terrible truth alone, she ncw continued her inquiry—

"But how would you reconcile such an affection with the vow of chastity which, as a novice, I have solemnly taken ?"

"It needs but little reconciliation, daughter," said he, taking her fair hand into his own. "Thou art indeed under the three vows of poverty, chastity, and obedience ; yet thou mayst, by the law of obedience, be absolved from the law of poverty, and at the will of thy Superior become rich. If the temptation of riches lead thee to sin, it is his sin who commanded, not thine who obeyed ; for the law of obedience is superior to the law of poverty, and thou dost right, and the holy church will absolve thee from all sin in obeying. So with chastity. Now shouldst thou love the most pious young priest, and should he, which is not at all improbable, have the weakness to yield to the same irresistible affection, it would at least be a comfort to you to know that the sin would be ascribable to his weakness, for that you were bound to him by the vow of obedience, which is superior even to the vow of chastity."

"And would you, then, holy father, that I should transfer the affection I have borne for Walter to you and your good brothers ?"

"I would not willingly commit my brothers, or

speak for them without authority," said the priest, in a voice intended to be of the most seductive sweetness, but revolting to her from its excessive impudence. "But for myself," he continued, "such an affection would find in me a genial and happy sympathy."

While he yet spoke, and ere she was fully aware, the young father confessor had encircled her waist in his left arm, and with the other stayed her hand while he would have imprinted a kiss on her brow.

"No, priest!" she shrieked, recoiling, with a spring, from his hated grasp. "Wretch! fiend!—you who but wear the livery of angels to serve the devil in; the air is stifling in your presence. Let me away!" and hastily rising from her kneeling position, she rushed from the apartment.

Her resolution was immediately taken, and no sooner had she fled the presence of the unworthy one, than she sought in haste the room of the Mother Superior. She was admitted, and bowing with reverence as she passed through the door before the form of the blessed virgin, which stood in a niche in the wall, and kneeling and kissing the ground, as was usual, before the holy mother, she rose and requested leave to depart the institution on the following day.

The mother, who was a lady hardly above forty years of age, intellectual and somewhat handsome, with a smooth, agreeable voice, and a benignant manner, indicative rather of suavity than of real kindness, heard her request without any manifestation of surprise. She then enlarged, with much apparent kindness in her manner, upon the advantages and elevated pleasures of the life of a devoted recluse, contrasting them forcibly with the dangers and troubles which beset the woman of the world, adjured her not to take any such downward step, which she could only repent when too late, told her that the prayers of the sisterhood would be offered for her continuance in her present good life, and finally assured her that at ten o'clock on the morrow, were she then of the same resolution, she should return to the world as she had left it.

True to the hour, at ten o'clock on the morrow she was summoned into the presence of the Mother Superior. She felt, as she entered the room, that she was in the presence of another person, though from the habit, now grown familiar to her, of walking with her eyes fixed upon the ground, in token of humility, she saw or rather felt no more than his presence.

"Daughter," spoke the matron, as Julia rose from the usual prostrate salutation, "are you still of the same mind?"

"I still feel it my duty to go," replied Julia; "I would willingly devote myself to a life of charity, but my heart tells me that I may do so even beyond these walls."

"Of that," said the Mother Superior, "you may judge better hereafter, but as such is your resolution I can no longer, by a doubtful exercise of authority, endeavor to screen you from your proper and lawful condition. Mr. Preston," she said, addressing the stranger, "she is yours."

Julia started—a cold, shuddering chill shook her frame, and seemed to freeze the very currents of her heart. A frightful expression of terror distorted her countenance, and drops of the sweat of agony stood on her brow. For the first time in their lives the father and daughter glanced toward each other in the mutual consciousness of their real relation as master and slave. The owner shrunk abashed before the eagle glance of his high-souled chattel, while the latter fully realized that the tender cord of filial love in her own heart was at that instant cut—severed forever. Her expression of terror changed into one of heart-sickness and disgust, and as she met alternately his cowering eye, and the even more heartless calmness of the Sister of Charity, she felt as if all that was good and pure and worthy in her conceptions of the world, were now passing from under her feet, and ready to precipitate her into a boundless abyss.

CHAPTER XXV.

TO THE SLAVE-PEN.

" They mourn, but smile at length; and smiling mourn.
The tree will wither long before it fall;
The hull drives on though mast and sail be torn,
The roof-tree sinks but moulders on the hall
In massy hoariness: the ruined wall
Stands when its windworn battlements are gone;
The bars survive the captive they enthral;
The day drags through though storms keep out the sun;
And thus the heart will break, yet brokenly live on."
Childe Harold's Pilgrimage.

By the aid of an attendant, Julia, over whom the lethargic prostration of despair seemed for the time to brood, was borne rather than led to a carriage, which stood waiting at the street-gate, into which, scarcely sensible, she was deposited. During the last half hour there had protruded from the door of this carriage, in eager watchfulness, a lean, long, skinny and cadaverous face, shaded by a bushy growth of fiery yellow hair, and ornamented by two small and restless gray eyes, a nose which, in size and color resembled an inverted beet, and a hair-lip, the effect of which was heightened by a bristling moustache, which, totally undisciplined by the comb or adjusting finger, stood out in every direction like a Canada thistle.

"Guv -us yer pawr, Judy, an' don't whimper afore yer hurt nuther," said this head, as it withdrew into the carriage, allowing room for them to lift in the half-senseless Julia, in which operation the owner of the head assisted, by seizing both her arms in a very business-like way, and requesting those outside to "guv her a gentle boost, an' not hurt the gal," pursuant to which tender entreaty she was lifted into her seat.

"Wull neaow, friend Preston," said the lurid head, now widened by a broad grin of disgusting admiration, as he stared at Julia, "yer see, she arn't 'zackly wot I thot she waur, but howasever she's 'bout as likely a lookin' parcel as I've sold for some time. Yer see, Joe Swingler can't be cheated on a girl—he's bought and sold too many on 'em. I see her better and wors pints as quick as I woud a mare's."

Julia looked at the unsightly wretch before her with loathing and astonishment. She had not dreamed of the existence of such creatures.

"Be still, my honey—I arn't gwine to bruise yer. Yer as safe in Joe Swingler's hands as in most people's. Yer'll be fed purty well, and dressed nice, an' I guess yer won't be worked very hard—ha, ha, Judy, I guess yer won't be worked very hard. But, Mr.

Preston, arter all, her figger is mis'able. That is, it's neat and purty enough in a common way, but nuthin to what it might be. She's been on low diet among the nuns, an she wants fatten up. An then she's got the devil's own pluck, an it 'll be the job to break her in. Yer see——"

"Beg pardon, Mr. Swingler, I would rather talk with you of business, when we have more leisure," for even he blushed with shame, and hurriedly turned to depart.

"But, hold up, Preston—don't go off half cocked. Now my motto is 'bizness is bizness'—that's my maxim, friend Preston, an I swow it's a true one. 'Cordin'ly, yer see my rule is, when I am doin' a thing —to do it—don't yer see ?—and then when it's done it's done—and it never has to be done a second time, unless it's done so the first time, that it has to be done over agin—don't yer see ? Them's my conwictions, and what better can a man do than to foller his own conwictions—right and wrong—Mr. Preston. Now, as I was sayin'—various pints about the gal arn't purty, though they're tolable, and then her waist is too small altogether—although, I say again, she's considerable neat—but she won't bring nothing like the full thousand at a reg'lar sale. Take my word and sacred honor for that. Now, Preston, I'd like to 'commodate you with the money right off—wot d'ye say ? I won't deal close, seein' it's you, for I know it would be no go—so I'll come right up to the very highest mark at once," said he, producing a roll of bank bills and twirling them lightly and leisurely in his left hand. " Say five hundred and fifty, Mr. Preston? Not a cent more can you get by waiting till the day of judgment—and you know, Mr. Preston, you would'nt want to wait quite till that time to sell her."

" Positively," said Mr. Preston, " you must excuse my departure. " I have an engagement which I must keep. But less than the thousand I cannot think of taking. Good morning, Mr. Swingler."

" Hallo ! Say the even six hundred, Mr. Preston," said Swingler, darting his head out of the carriage window, and looking earnestly after the receding Mr. Preston, who bowed a negative, and turned again upon his heel. " Say six-fifty ; seven hundred, Preston—seven hundred," he bawled, " cash down. I say, hold on, Preston—I'll go the eight now. Never'll give as much again to save your soul from h—— !"

In justice to the various charitable and kindly qualities of Mr. Swingler, we should state that the peroration of this amiable exhortation was not intended to hurt the feelings of Mr. Preston, but purely to relieve his own, as they were uttered in so low a voice, the golden head and lustrous nose receding into the carriage at the time, as never to reach the unsuspecting ears of his friend Preston.

The driver cracked his whip, and the hack was splashed through the mud, and walked over the dry pavement in the usual style and pace of worn-out nags, whose owners consider whips cheaper than oats.

What, during that brief ride, were the sensations of that proudly intellectual, superbly beautiful, and thrillingly spiritual chattel, as she thus confronted the vile and soulless merchant dealer, upon whose counter her life, hopes, and destiny were about to be laid for bargain and sale ! Oh, reader, have you ever subtly philosophized upon the inequalities among mankind, which render the subordination of the lower to the higher orders necessary, and therefore just ? Look into that carriage ; behold the inequality, and ask yourself if it justifies the " subordination."

After a short drive, by which Julia was, in part, restored to the possession of her scattered senses, the carriage halted before a neat, plain building, apparently a dwelling, and having nothing peculiar in its outward appearance to indicate that it was otherwise, except the number of careless, jaunty scrutinizers who thronged in the hall and around the doorway. But Julia recoiled instinctively as the steps were let down, for she felt that with her entrance into this place, the first poisoned barb of the inquisitorial machine would penetrate and fester in her soul.   But she mustered courage and descended.   As she did so, a crowd of peering faces, all distorted by equally disgusting expressions, vulgar interest, and lewd admiration, crowded around her.

"There's a beauty for you," said Swingler, with a business nod, wink, and smile.   "Pick her up, boys, and bring her in," he continued ; for at this moment Julia—her face livid and moistened with agony, every lineament quivering with deep, unutterable woe—had sunk in the grasp of her supporters upon the earth, and raising her clasped hands, had prayed, (a whim not unusual with slaves on such occasions.)

"Oh, good Father ! let me die.   Oh, Lord Jesus ! will you not take me !   Holy Virgin !   Oh, oh—let me die !"

"Never mind the Lord Jesus, Judy ; I'm inclined to think he don't keep this place.   Call on Joe Swingler," urged that worthy gentleman, in hilarious mockery.   "He can help you.   And as for holy virgins, they've sometimes been here, but they didn't remain here long.   They're a kind of thing we don't believe in."   These happy hits were received by the bystanders with appreciating laughter, and he continued : "There, boys, don't muss her feathers ; she's too nice a bird to be roughly handled.   Put her in number fourteen ; there's only three women and a boy in there now.—

By the limpin' Jove ! if they can sell that critter for a quadroon, I'd like to know why I couldn't sell my wife, born in the State of Vermont, of an English mam and a Scotch dad, and as brown as a mouse, for a pure mulatto ? By the limpin' Jove ! I wish I had her here ; I'd try it."

While this affectionate allusion to the loved but absent Mrs. Swingler was being uttered, Julia was led, in a bewildered trance, through the hall, at the end of which an iron-grated door creaked fearfully after her, and across a wide court surrounded by high brick walls, and in the centre of which was a small raised platform, and up a staircase, and along a corridor to the designated cell. Again a heavy grated iron door creaked fearfully upon its hinges—she entered. The door closed upon her, and the sound of the bolt of the lock, as it was moved into its place by the key— that most dismal of all sounds, save the falling of the earth upon the coffin of a living man—was heard, and Julia Preston, sitting down upon a rude pallet of straw, upon the other side of which a drunken negro was sitting, looked around at the four walls of her cell in the slave jail.

CHAPTER XXVI.

REVELATIONS.

" 'Tis then delightful misery no more,
But agony unmixed, incessant gall,
Corroding every thought, and blasting all
Love's paradise. Ye fairy prospects, then,
Ye beds of roses, and ye bowers of joy,
Farewell ! ye gleamings of departed peace,
Shine out your last ! the yellow-tinging plague
Internal vision taints, and in a night
Of livid gloom imagination wraps.
Ah then ! instead of love, enlivened cheeks,
Of sunny features and of ardent eyes
With flowing rapture bright, dark looks succeed
Suffused and glaring with untender fire ;
A clouded aspect and a burning cheek,
Where the whole poisoned soul malignant sits,
And frightens love away."   THOMSON

LET us return for a few moments to the " Flying
Scud." Within the same little cabin in which we
have already witnessed an interview between Lafitte
and Conrad, the former has been seated for a time,
with several letters and a heavy pistol before him—
alone and in thought. But now he rings, with his
usual impatience, a bell which lies upon the table, and

which is answered in a moment by the appearance of Annette.

" Conrad," snarled the pirate laconically, for he was in one of his thoughtful moods, " call him."

" He is more pleasantly engaged in sighing and simpering over his new conquest," replied Annette; " of course you would not have me disturb him."

" Wench, call him instantly !" growled Lafitte in a tone that precluded any further display of flippancy on her part, and Annette vanished to obey the summons. The cabins of the vessel being connected by a single passage-way, a step brought her to the door of Ada. She knocked, and Ada's soft voice answered—

" Come in, dear !"

Ada was standing in the centre of the room. A loose gown of white muslin fell like a drapery over her beautiful form, unconfined save at the waist by the encircling arm of Mr. Howard, or, as the reader already perceives him to be—*Conrad Defoe.* Her right hand yielded fondly to the pressure of his remaining one, while her other rested affectionately, and, it seemed pleadingly, upon his shoulder.

" Dearest Arthur," she murmured, the presence of Annette indicates that it is not safe for you to remain longer ; and yet it seems as if I cannot part from you, even for a few hours. Oh, Arthur !"

" My own Ada !" said Mr. Howard, while a tear

that trembled upon his lid coursed down and fell upon her cheek, as he drew her still closer to his bosom, and bending over pressed a kiss upon her upturned lips. "Dearest Ada, for a brief time shall the sweets of love be thus marred, but fear not. Soon, very soon, we shall be delivered from the evil wretches into whose hands we have fallen. Good-bye, dearest Ada!"

The girl still hung fondly and passionately upon his arm, as if she feared to release her hold upon it.

"Good-bye, Ada!" he repeated, gently releasing himself, and again imprinting upon her fair, pale brow, the pledge of his affection.

Annette, who had returned to the outside of the door, as if to watch against foreign interruption, and upon whose countenance a bitter, malignant smile had alternated with the scowl of hatred as one or the other of the lovers had spoken, now re-opened it, and entered with a face wrought with marvellous quickness into a sweet smile, mingled with apprehension and fear, and whispered hurriedly—

"Positively, Mr. Howard, you will be discovered if you delay a moment longer. I am sure your sweet little wife will excuse you, after enjoying your company so long," she said, embracing Ada and kissing her, "what more could you ask, little charm?"

"Only that," replied Ada coaxingly, as she followed Mr. Howard to the door, and again reposed her clasped hands affectionately upon his manly bosom, "only that you too should call me by that same endearing term."

Mr. Howard folded her clinging form once more in his embrace, and whispered in her ear the sweet, small word, "*wife*," kissed her affectionately, and slowly withdrawing from her embrace left the room with Annette, leaving the confiding Ada full of varied emotions, and reflecting upon a flood of recent experiences which she could scarcely realize, but on the whole happy.

"It was hard for me to call her wife in your presence," said Conrad, when the door had closed, enfolding Annette in his arms, and kissing her with less of passion and more of familiarity than he had lately shown: "I could not have done so, had you not compelled me to—"

"Ah, no! I suppose not," said Annette, with an attempted sneer, though pleased in spite of herself with his dalliance. "But it is entirely unnecessary for you to ply your art of flattery upon me. I am yours without that trouble. Besides, you know that I place not the slightest confidence in your expressions of regard. Oh, would for our poor sex that honest men, if there are such, could win our love as easily as rogues."

"What does the old devil want of me?" whispered

Conrad, sharply, as they halted before the door of Lafitte's cabin.

"The devil knows, ask him," replied Annette, opening the door and entering the cabin.

"We want to plan," said Lafitte, with the same terse fierceness as before, indicating that his dark spirit was more than usually troubled. "Wench, leave!"

"I have the same interest in the success of your projects that you have, and my judgment is probably as good," replied Annette, calmly, seating herself, "and I prefer to stay."

With equal calmness the pirate took up the loaded pistol from the table, shook it gently, examined the priming, and then aimed it at the girl, and pulled the trigger. It snapped. Except the slight nervous twich that stirred her, she flinched not. He pulled back the trigger again, aimed and drew, but again it snapped.

"Have you concluded to go?" thundered the pirate, in a tone like the growl of the lion when he vaults upon his prey.

"No, captain Lafitte."

"Fiends in h——, you havn't, eh? Get me another pistol then," he yelled with still more terrible fierceness.

"I shall do nothing of the kind," replied Annette calmly.

His face, now livid with supprest but almost bursting rage, the pirate, with a tremulous hand which his forced calmness would not render steady, once more knocked the breech violently, adjusted the priming, and taking a steady aim, pulled the trigger. Again it snapped. Again she flinched not. Circumstances for which the astonished outlaw might have more easily accounted had he witnessed Annette half an hour before when she withdrew the charge and dampened the priming.

"Child of the devil—do you want me to shoot you ?"

"I do !" replied Annette, "exactly."

"Oh, eh ! you do indeed," said the pirate, in a quieted tone, flinging the pistol into a corner, and for some whim, best known to himself, changing his purpose. "Well, sit where you are. I will wait then till some time when you don't. Conrad," said he, taking up a letter before him, " I have been offered by Pakenham the rank of Captain in the royal navy, and the sum of" (and here his voice sunk as he named the reward into a low whisper inaudible even to Annette) " to furnish him with all the information he wants relative to New Orleans, and to assist him in taking the place."

" Better not accept it," remarked Annette, quietly.

" Devil's own hound," yelled the pirate chief, now

fully enraged. " Speak again, woman, and you die !
What do you think of the proposition ?" he continued, returning to Conrad, with a fierceness scarcely
abated.

" Friends," said Annette, advancing and laying the
tips of her fingers upon the table, upon opposite sides
of which they were sitting. " For once I shall advise
you, whether you choose to follow my advice or not.
You cannot float much longer unhung in your present
business.   Not only these parts but the world is getting
too hot to hold you.   With the close of this war you
will be immediately hunted down and destroyed.   Besides, how can you wish to die as pirates, when you
are rich enough to buy a principality and live as
princes ? Mark my words, Jean Lafitte, you had
better go back and live an honest blacksmith by ham-
mering at your old anvil in New Orleans, than to continue longer in your present business.   America is,
after all, your country, and the only one that will dare
protect you.   If you are going to show the white
feather, you might as well surrender to your friends
as your enemies.   You have the power, by exposing
the whole of this diabolical scheme, to do your country a great service.   Do so, and she will receive you
with open arms—if not respectable, at least pardoned.
I have said all I mean to say, and have done my duty.

Live or die, I am with you. I leave you to reflect upon this and form your own conclusion."

This saying, she retired, while the two pirates, not a little astonished at so strange and unaccustomed a demonstration, stared at each other in silence. Conrad first broke the spell.

"It strikes me that the——"

"Girl is right," interrupted Lafitte, with an emphasis from the fierceness of which his vein of admiration for the heroine did not detract. "The girl is right," he repeated, bringing his huge fist down upon the table with a force that seemed adequate to shiver it to atoms.

"For once I take counsel of a woman"

CHAPTER XXVII.

A HEROIC ACHIEVEMENT.

"A kind of change came in my fate;
My keepers grew compassionate:
I know not what had made them so
They were inured to sights of woe;
But so it was."   THE PRISONER OF CHILLON.

WHILE the events recorded in the few last chapters were transpiring, an enterprise profoundly interesting to the person most concerned, was approaching its issue. A short time was to decide whether this was to be added to the long list of heroic and skillful achievements over which the magic wand of success has dropped the unfading wreath of glory, or whether it, like many others equally well devised, was to be stamped by failure with the brand of demerit, thence to sink into undisturbed oblivion, or to be remembered only with untimely levity ; for while it may sometimes be true that the hero makes success, it is invariably true that success makes the hero.

Had we followed Sandy and the unceremonious stranger in half uniform who so summarily introduced himself to his acquaintance at the quay, we should have inferred that nothing short of the fastidious politeness in which, as a family servant of the Prestons, Alexander had been educated, could have induced him to follow, without dissent, the route pursued by his newly fledged acquaintance. By whatever motive actuated, however, he did so, and the result was that Sandy had been for several weeks contemplating, with the most unphilosophical want 'of serenity, the iron-grated door, hard plank bed, four walls, ceiling and floor of his little box-like cell in the city prison. There was, indeed, one small, closely grated window, very high up, in one side of his cell, through which opened a heavenly prospect of inconceivable dimensions, the value of which Sandy's limited amount of astronomical knowledge did not enable him fully to appreciate. Occasionally during the long nights, a twinkling star would come within the range of his vision through this loop-hole, which Sandy would watch until it would pass into a total eclipse behind one of the bars, and then until it would come out again and pass behind another, so that Sandy was not entirely without amusement.

He was the possessor of a jack-knife ; and had he also possessed a stick upon which to use it, or a piece of chalk and the liberty to mark upon the walls, or a smooth, round stone, which he could have tossed from one hand to the other through the livelong day, he would have been tolerably happy. Especially could he have monopolized a jews'-harp or a violin, he would have been secure against monotony. But neither of these were his. Occasionally the keeper vouchsafed a grateful quid of tobacco, and twice Alexander had gloried in a segar. But with these slight exceptions, he had been thrown for his entertainment and relief from the monotonous tedium incident to his limited quarters and select society, entirely upon his own tact, talents, and abilities. Sometimes he would tie his legs in a hard knot, and walk around his cell three times upon his hands ; then he would whistle for an hour, and occupy himself in conversation with imaginary spectators ; then he would fling his pedestals in the air, until his feet would graze along the sky of his little world, or perhaps rest against it ; and there he would stand with his hands upon the floor, and his feet upon the ceiling, as if he had forgotten which way the attraction of gravitation worked, until one would have thought he had gone to sleep ; then he would whistle again ; then he would join his hands in front of him, and jump over them, and then whistle violently.

But notwithstanding these and many other performances so interesting as to be repeated again and again, it would be vain to say that Sandy was not, on the whole, weary of his new way of life.

" Sandy," said he to himself one day, after a long revery, "Sandy, sit down here on dis bed; I'm gwine to talk to you like a fader."

So Sandy sat down upon the hard pallet, and proceeded to listen to his own fatherly discourse.

" Sandy, you're a rascal—you're de greatest rascal out o' jail; no, you ain't out o' jail. Beg pardon, Sandy. I wish de Lor' you was—you are de greatest rascal in jail. I specs dere may be some greater rascals out o' jail dan you are. Kaze why—if dere hadn't been, you wouldn't a been in jail. So dat's clar. But, nebberdeless, Sandy, you're a rascal. You whimp an' say, ' Now, done say dat to Sandy, I neber means to do nuffin' wrong.'

" So much de wos for ye. You's wos 'n dat. You's onlucky. Now, Sandy, I neber thought dat o' you. I know you'd steal oats, but dat's nuffin' so long as you was lucky—massa neber kotch you. I know you lie, but dat ars nuffin' unless you are onlucky in get found out. But if you's onlucky, I'm down on yer.

" Now, Sandy, jis look at it, an' if you'll hark to reason I'll 'splain it to you. Friend Sandy, if you had only bin stealin' oats twice, an' not got kotched, an' den steal oats once more, an' jis as you goin' out wid de oats, de dog's teeth stick like a poor nigger's plaster to de small o' your back, an' you bawl an' bawl till massa come and say, 'Sandy, you take twenty lashes jis where de dog bit yer,' or, 'Sandy, you go to jail till I git time to lick yer,' I feel in my heart like sayin', 'Tankee, massa,' because Sandy been lucky, Sandy got off cleah twice, an' you, massa, try bery hard an' jis make out to kotch him once. But now, Sandy, you 'fernal rascal, I'd like to know what got you here but onluckiness. How many times, on dis 'tickler 'casion, did you do somefin' bad an' go cleah? None at all. You did nuffin' bad as you knows on. An' heah you be in jail, you 'fernal rascal. You's de greatest rascal I know—you's was. You's onlucky enough to be hung some day, an' you will be hung. Now, Sandy, mark my words, you'll be hung, not because you's bad, but because you's onlucky. Sandy, I'm down on you, I'm ashamed of you. Sandy, good-bye, I cut youah 'quaintance jis as I would cut any friend as was on- lucky—until he got out o' trouble."

What might have been the lamentable consequences of Sandy's positive refusal to have anything more to do with himself, we are happily prevented from know- ing, for just at this critical moment, as if through his widely-opened mouth a flood of light had suddenly poured in upon his brain, Sandy sprung to the floor, stood a moment in dreamy thought, looked out of the little grated window, whistled a long, shrill blast, and then, after several unwieldy somersets and other gymnastic performances, having somewhat shaken off his joy, sat calmly down and held his sides and laughed with a low, quiet, cunning chuckle.

"No, Sandy, you's mighty smart—Sandy, you's lucky—I'll stand up for you, Sandy, after all—you've got it now, Sandy, good for you—good boy, good boy !"

So saying, Sandy put up both hands and patted himself on the back twice, in token of his high appreciation of the talents which nature had enriched him with, and of the wonderful perfection to which they had been developed by education.

In a few minutes the warden's wife appeared, to hand to Sandy, through the slide in the grated door, his unsavory dinner.

"Please, missus," said Sandy in a voice of pleading humility, "I so dirty I can't feel no consolation o' religion. I'se so dirty makes me feel wicked. Now, if missus hab de kind consequentiousness on a poor nigger as has seen better days, to send him a tub o' water, to bathe and cleansify his ole duds with, he save missus de trouble o' havin' 'em washed, an' to-morrow he come out clean an' nice, an' he feel like tankin' missus an' prayin' for de Lord to permit an' pardon his sins."

Whether it was to deliver poor Sandy from his wickedness, or to save herself from trouble, or on account of the touching character of the whole appeal, the matron promised assent.

"Please, missus," said Sandy as she was leaving.

"What more do you want?"

"Please, missus, a good big tub, for Sandy am bery fond ob his bath."

The articles were soon brought, to the satisfaction of Sandy, who, as the door again closed on him and the porters disappeared, mentally rewarded them by placing his finger at the base of his broad, flat nose, and leering quizzically after them.

No sooner had they retired, than Sandy commenced operation; carefully donning his own garments, which had been temporarily provided him for the purpose, he hurriedly ran his prison apparel through the water, and hung the latter upon a string which he had attached to two nails, driven in the mortar of the wall. When he had thus suspended them, he proceeded very industriously to remove, by the aid of his jack-knife, the mortar from around the small wedge stones which held fast one of the heaviest stones in the wall, immediately behind one of the garments he had washed. In a few moments, with some labor, these little stones and much mortar were removed, and carefully put to soak in the suds which his recent cleansing operations had made opaque with dirt. Soon the great stone be-gan to loosen, and in an hour it also was safely deposited in the tub, where the water rose over it and it was invisible. Thus he labored until the first faint beam of light shone through the orifice, and then waited until the warden's man entered with his evening meal. Sandy's apparent work then fell down over his real labors, and when the warden's man asked him what he was doing, he pointed to the tub and to the shirt upon the wall, and said with a grin—

"Don't yer see, massr, Sandy wants to come out clean if he can."

The warden's man smiled good-naturedly, and departed. Sandy jumped up immediately, and, as it was now twilight, silently and cautiously removed stone after stone and laid them on the floor, as concealment of his work would have been no longer possible. When the orifice was large enough to admit his shoulders he looked out, to his infinite gratification, upon a narrow alley, lined with stables. There was not a person in sight. Half an hour more he worked industriously, and again looked forth. He was in the second story of the building, but all beneath was wrapped in auspicious silence and repose. In a trice he had leaped to the ground, and the dawn of the next morning found him pursuing the even tenor of his way to Lindenhall, occasionally ejaculating, "Sandy, you's mighty smart—Sandy, you's lucky."

CHAPTER XXVIII.

THE HERO RETURNED.

Sandy dared not approach nearer to Lindenhall, but lurking in the chapparel till dusk, he then approached the hut of old Tim and Aunt Tanzey, which stood, fortunately, upon the very outskirts of the quarters.

"Why, de Lor' bless your dear soul, honey," exclaimed old Aunt Tanzey, seizing him in her arms with a heartiness of embrace worthy of her younger days, as soon as she recognized him, while the tears chased each other down her cheeks. "Lor' bless us, if it arn't Sandy, for all de worl'—true as Gospel. Sandy Preston—my eyes—is it you? du tell. Now for de Lor's sake, do tell us what's happened and what's goin' to happen. Is the world comin' to an end? Did you eber! If my old Tim ain't jis done gone up to de Hall—and dare dey be—all de week holden meetin' and prayin' and shoutin', for old Tim says de debil's comin' now for all on us—an I b'lieve he is. But we'd all gin you up for dead and gone, and jes' now as I was a mixin de biscuit for poor old Tim, who keeps a sayin', now, Tanzey, dere's no use for to mix it, for it'll burn afore mornin'—and I says, No it won't burn afore mornin', for I won't put it on de fire till mornin'—and he says—says he—Tanzey, I say unto you, verily, de debil will put us all on de fire afore mornin'—for de worl' aint goin' to last annuder day.   Well, as I was sayin', jis as I was mixin' ob de biscuit, as poor Tim talks so about—who should come in but Sandy Preston.   Now, Sandy, can't yer tell us somefin' about Miss July and Miss Ady?   You always knows ebberyting."

"De Lor' sakes," said Sandy, " you don't tell me anythin's happened to dem angels—do ye ?"

"Don't tell yer.   And 'av I got to tell yer ?   Yer poor, miserable, ignorum, runaway wagabone—has ye been down in de big swamp dis seven week—or whar has ye been, dat ye ain't heerd what de whole libbin world is cryin' an goin' on about ?   Ain't der a foren army around de city goin' to take it, and ain't it highly possible dat de whole world'll burn up unless Misses July and Miss Ady brought back soon, an' you ain't heerd nuffin' about it ?   Whar you been, you igno-rum scamp ?—down in de swamp ?—you wagabone. De Lor' blastize us dat we didn't set de dogs on yer. We might a knowed you was dare."

"Hush, Aunt Tanzey," said Sandy with assumed dignity—"I tell yer I ain't been in de big swamp."

"Wot a lie, you waga——"

"No, Aunt Tanzey," continued Sandy, bridling— "Ise been in de calaboose all dis time, an ain't eat nuffin' for two days an nights—an now I've got into old Tim's cabin at last, I didn't spec to be 'bused quite dis way."   And what with fright at the news which had just broken upon him, together with his exhaustion and his real grief at the unwelcome animadversions of Aunt Tanzey, Sandy sunk upon a stool, covered his face with his hands and wept.

This was too much for the really kind-hearted old negress.

"Why, de Lor' bress yer deah soul, honey—don't go on so !" she said, as kneeling before him and loosening her bunch of gray wool from the folds of her red bandana handkerchief, she applied it in a motherly way to his eyes.   "I did'n mean nuffin'.   Only I thort you might tell somefin' about de poor los' angels, God bless 'em.   I fraid we neber heah nuffin' more good bout dem in dis worl, an we be mighty sure we neber heah nuffin' bad in de nex'."

"Neber hear from dem ar—wat yer mean, Aunt Tanzey ?" exclaimed Sandy.

"Woll now, you poor soul, I tell yer.   Poor Miss July, an' dat ar strange gemman o' hers, an' you, all

went off onbeknown to no one, de same night, leavin'
poor Miss Ady all alone ; an' sez I to ole Tim, sez I,
'.Tim, de nex' ting be Miss Ady.'   An' sure enough,
de bery nex' day Miss Ady nowhar to be diskibbered,
'dough we all scour up an' down, high an' low, and
look nine ways for Sunday.   An' Massa Preston hardly
been here since ; an' dey say we're all gwine to be sole
off agin, if we ain't sole off already, for de hall, an'
de niggers, an' eberyting is all gone to de new owner.
Dey call him Iasaacks, I b'leeb, an' his ole lantern-
jawed, slinkey-slawney lawyer's been up here.   Dey
call him Snakes, and he looks enough like 'em, I'm
sure.

"So ye see, all de Prestons is goin' right down in
de worl', right down to nuffin', an' we're gwine to be
sole, one one way an' anoder anoder ; so we must
make up our minds all to part soon, to meet no more
on dis side Jordan.   Oh, poor Tim," wept the old
negress, " poor Tim, what will 'com' ob him ?"

" Lor' sakes ! ain't it too bad ?" blubbered Sandy.
"But whar de Lor' sakes Miss July an' Miss Ady
gone ?"

" Whar am dey ! Ax de moon. She's de only one
we know dat's seen 'em.   Dead or libin', weal or woe,
not a libin' soul knows wot's happened 'em," sobbed
the old lady, while the hot tears, thicker and faster

with every word she uttered, coursed down the face of honest Sandy.

" So yer see, bless yer, honey, I was only a little nat'-ral pervoke like when I foun' yer didnt know nuffin'. So don' go on so now, God bless yer. But wot de Lor' sakes ye been to de calaboose for ?   Wot ye did ? Ye kilt anybody ?   Don' tell me de stain o' blood on yer, Sandy."

" No, no, Tanzey."

"Anybody kilt *dem*—murdered *dem!*   Say, Sandy, yer wagabone, wot yer been to de calaboose for ?"

" I habn't de leas' inception," replied Sandy.

" Wot's dat mean ?   Speak plain, an' no big words, Sandy.   Ise no larnin, I tell yer ; an' while you'm makin' up some lie or oder, I'll git yer some supper, for yer looks as if yer hadn' eat a mouthful sin' yer been hidin' away in de swamp ; an' I done b'leeb yer hab."

" I dun no wot I ben to calaboose for. How should I know ?" said Sandy.

" Dun no !"

" No."

" Mus' ben some reason, else how come yer in ?"

" 'Cos I was onlucky, I 'speck," replied Sandy.

"An' how come ye out ?"

" 'Cos I was lucky agin, I 'speck," said Sandy.

"Did you eber!" exclaimed Aunt Tanzey, in amaze-
ment.

"No, I neber!" rejoined Sandy, by which exclama-
·tions the impression was mutually arrived at that
events had at last become to them too wonderful to
admit of narration, much less of explanation.

CHAPTER XXIX.

"POOR ADA.'

> ' The storm is stilled.
> Father in heaven ! Thou, only thou, canst sound
> The heart's great deep, with floods of anguish filled,
> For human line too fearfully profound.
> Therefore, forgive, my Father ! if thy child,
> Rocked on its heaving darkness hath grown wild,
> And sinned in her despair ! It well may be
> That thou wouldst lead my spirit back to thee
> By the crushed hope too long in this world poured,
> The stricken love which hath perchance adored
> A mortal in thy place ! Now let me strive
> With thy strong arm no more ! Forgive, forgive !
> Take me to peace."   MRS. HEMANS.

IT was on the eve of the memorable eighth of January, 18—. Ada was watching from the window of her cabin prison the last rays of the declining sun, as they cast their bright golden sheen over the calm waters of the Mississippi, for the boundless expanse of ocean was no longer before her, but the distant line of low, flat, interminable marshes and lagoons which surround the outlets of that noble river, formed the horizon. Her little chin reposed in a revery, which seemed to be one of sadness, upon her left hand. In her right was a small miniature—in her eye a tear. Whose is the miniature—and whose the tear? The features of the former are those of Mr. Howard! Ada, gentle Ada, what change hath passed over thee since we saw thee last? Wreathe once more the fond smile of infantile innocence, that we may see thee now as first at Lindenhall. Look not so desponding, heart-sick, and weary. Thine eye hath lost its serene joy, and beams with a restless lustre. Why start with every gentle breath of air, why flutter with every foot-step, why, trembling, echo so mournfully as from an over-burdened breast the melancholy sighs of the night wind? Where have thy joy and peace flown—and why doth this insane unrest speak in every feature and every action, as if it oppressed heavily thy soul? Oh, Ada, Ada, tearful Ada, thou seest the angels weeping for thee. See, she sighs. Ah, that sigh!

"Will he never—never come?"

For some time after the departure of Ada and her lover from the Festal Island, the latter had been even more constant than ever before in his visits. When he was present, her waking hours flew away uncounted in a dream of pleasure, which she neither seemed to have power to weigh or to control. During his short absences the recollection of the recent past, the anticipation of the near future, left little time for painful reflection, and the gentle Ada borrowed from his influence a new nature, which, though foreign to her for the time, sat upon the throne of her soul, and swayed her emotions as he listed.

But gradually his visits grew less frequent, his caresses less endearing, his enjoyment less evident. During these absences the demon Sorrow, in dark robes and mournful aspect, stalked like a spectre into the dimly-lighted chamber of her soul, and sat in the chair· of Joy. Accusations, distrust, and jealousy chilled their meetings, and their vows of love trembled as they were uttered, with the weight of their own falsehood. Let us not further draw aside the veil. The rest was wretchedness and woe unutterable.

A gentle rap at the door jars her shattered nerves as if it were an earthquake, and, rising hastily, she adjusts her bosom-pin, and twining a stray ringlet before the mirror, says softly—

"Come in !"

The door opens—" Ah, is it you, Annette ?"

"Yes, poor dear," said Annette with a smile, " I am sorry it is no other, but he cannot come with safety within an hour. We are very near to the city. A great excitement is tumbling everything upside down, as if they were preparing to board an Indiaman, and Lafitte dashes in and out of his cabin every minute."

"How strange, Annette, that this wild crew should have caged me here so long, and that I should never have seen aught of any of them ; when will this terrible dream pass away?" said Ada, trembling and weeping, for of late it was difficult for her to speak many sentences without a burst of tears.

"Do not cry, child," said Annette, as she kissed the weeping girl with a touch of real feeling, "you will soon be ransomed."

Annette retired and the door closed, but the words she had uttered sent a thrill to the childish heart of the simple girl to whom they were spoken. Drawing a cross from her bosom, she knelt before it and clasped her hands, but she could not pray. The words of prayer seemed to have been stricken from her memory, and the spirit of prayer banished from her soul. But in the low and incoherent accents of deepest woe, we can distinguish the words—

"Ransomed ! Oh, that I might be one of the ransomed ! But that will never be."

At last she rose, and looking a moment around her little boudoir, now wrapped in the shadows of twilight, she placed her finger upon the latch.

"Death," she whispered, "is better than this terrible suspense. What terrors can there be in danger to one who longs for death ? He fears to come to me—I will go to him."

Feeling her way cautiously along the passage, her attention was in a moment arrested by the deep, ponderous tones of him whose voice carried her back to the scene of her abduction from Lindenhall. A blank paleness flashed across her face as she heard, in earnest conversation with that rude, brutal voice, the rich, melodious, generous tones of Mr. Howard, and the voice also of Annette.

"Friends," said the latter, "you have now thrown yourselves too far into this breach either to falter or refuse. You have made a bargain, as men of honor, with a man of honor. Depend upon it, he will fulfil it if you will ; and he can now seize and hang you if you show a mind not to act up to your promise.— Hitherto you have sailed the seas with the brand of Cain on your brows ; your hands have been against every man, and every man's hand against you. Seize upon this opportunity which the American general has offered you of washing out, in their eyes, your past offences in the blood of their enemies."

"Bravo !" spoke that familiar voice, which never failed to send a thrill of pleasure or of pain to the heart of Ada.

"I don't know but it's as well," growled Lafitte. "Our men would fight in a breach like tigers at bay, so that at all events old Jackson will know enough not to hang us till the battle's over."

"And now," said Annette, "that father Reilly here has done so much to save our necks from the halter, and, if possible, our souls from hell, by being the bearer of such dangerous messages, but one service remains by which he can increase the debt of our—at least, Conrad, of *our* gratitude ?"

"What is that ?" replied the smooth tones of Mr. Howard, revealing to Ada's poor, desolated heart for the first time, as if the light of hell had shone in upon it, what he was, and therefore all that she had been. Sustained in consciousness by the intensity of her agony, she listened still.

"To marry us," replied Annette, firmly. From to-morrow's work we may never return alive. If you die, I die with you. If you live, I am still yours. But this late act of justice—you will not refuse it, Conrad ? I know you will not."

"A sorry wedding that !" said Conrad, with a scornful laugh. "As well might this priest's chattei attempt to change water into wine, as undertake, at this late hour, to hallow our relation."

"Oh, God !" groaned Ada, "is this him whom I have loved ?"

She heard the low, measured murmur of the priest, as he read the holy ceremony of the church. Trembling, she sunk upon her knees. A shriek quivered each moment upon her lips, but she suppressed it ;

and crawling back to her room, threw herself, exhausted and almost senseless, upon her couch.

That wild shriek was still in her heart, ready every moment to burst with the intensity of her passion.— Ever and anon it came to her lips, but still it hung there, till drivelling insanity shone in the fierce glare of her once mild and beautiful orbs ; yet she did not, could not utter it. But when Conrad entered her room, and she felt, though she could not see through the darkness, that he was present, that long, wild, demoniac shriek of desperation and woe, such as none but seducers hear, and all but devils pity, told him that his victim had at last read to the end of the chapter of his villany. He stood stricken for a moment, as he had often stood before—not with astonishment, but with deep, heartfelt grief, at the terrible results of his dexterous and heartless wickedness. Agitated, and trembling almost as violently as the poor being who had thrown herself at his feet, while the tears of involuntary penitence rolled for a moment, thick and fast, down his cheeks, he murmured—

"I cannot ask you to forgive me : God—if there is a God—will not. But, oh ! I am weaker than you. Pity me, pity me, Ada ; do not hate, but pity me !"

Strange power ! as he lifted up all that remained of the once angelic and high-souled Ada, she involuntarily gasped—

"No, Arthur—I cannot hate you. I do pity both of us. May God and the angels do likewise."

"Ada," he exclaimed, striving to suppress his emotion, "have you a—a last request—for we meet no more—forever."

A long silence followed, during which the poor girl stood trembling, leaning upon his arm, as she had so often done in happier hours. At last she spoke :

" My home !"

" Would you see it ?"

" Do not take me there—do not let them see their lost Ada. No, the lowest of them are princes and angels beside me. Do not let me stain the threshold. Nor my heavenly sister—I cannot meet her glance.— Let me have one last, long look—from the distance— from the river."

Uttering this with frequent sobbings, she permitted the last unholy kiss to be imprinted upon her pallid brows. * * * *

The midnight moon shone down with that noonday clearness and brilliancy, by which she sometimes strives to combine the splendor of the day with the loveliness of night, wrapping the whole earth in her soft mantle of light and glory. Ada was alone, looking thoughtfully, tearfully, sorrowfully, forth from her little cabin window, over the smooth moonlit waters of the Mississippi, upon the home of her infancy—the scene of

her childish sports and girlish innocence. There were
the same old cypresses, willows and cottonwood, scattered in groves and clusters, and robed in the beauty
of night, as she had often watched them from yonder
chamber window in the serenely contemplative, dreamy
hours of her girlhood.

. Thick and fast fell her tears, as she heard the an-
chor drop from the bow of the vessel, and for the first
time since she had been ruthlessly torn away from
that happy home, to roam a prisoner upon the bounding wave, a loved and familiar scene was again before
her, calm and motionless, inviting bitter, bitter reflection.

The hours wore away. It was near morning, and still
she remained wrapt in that tearful, sorrowful revery.
Suddenly she recovered her consciousness, and kneeling before her crucifix, she faintly endeavored to whisper words of prayer. Then rising, she stepped to the
open window, and took one last, long, tearful gaze at
the starry heavens above her, at the old home of her
childish days so full in view, and down at the calm,
deep waters that rolled sluggishly by, and ere another
moment passed, she had consigned her frail form,
without a sigh, without a murmur, to the waves.

> " One more unfortunate,
> Weary of breath,
> Rashly importunate
> Gone to her death."

From the deck of the vessel, in a dark and gloomy mood, with folded arms and knit brows, Conrad Defoe watched her golden hair, as it floated down with the current, and for a moment its streaming ringlets lingered and played upon the surface.   There was a faint struggle, as if the poor maiden would have risen to snatch one more glance at the home of her infancy, and then she sank—to rise no more.

He saw it, and sighed—

" Poor—poor—Ada !"

CHAPTER XXX.

AN EVENTFUL DAY.

> " Give order that these bodies
> High on a stage be placed to the view;
> And let me speak, to the yet unknowing world,
> How these things came about : So shall you hear
> Of carnal, bloody, and unnatural acts ;
> Of accidental judgments, casual slaughters ;
> Of deaths put on by cunning and forced cause ;
> And in this upshot, purposes mistook
> Fall'n on the inventors' heads."
>
> HAMLET, PRINCE OF DENMARK.

THE next morning, at an hour even earlier than usual, Sister Clara, emerging from the gate of the house of the Sisters with her little basket upon her arm, and following precisely the same route in which we have once before accompanied her, passed mechanically and without appearing to notice her way, through the same low streets into the narrow, filthy alley which led to the house of Iasaacks. The streets did not wear the lifeless and silent aspect usual at this early hour, but were full of the evidences of stirring action, excitement and anxiety, if not of fear.

" And there was mounting in hot haste; the steed,
  The mustering squadron, and the clattering car,
Went pouring forward with impetuous speed,
  And swiftly forming in the ranks of war ;
  And the deep thunder, peal on peal afar,
And near, the beat of the alarming drum,
  Roused up the soldier ere the morning star ,
While thronged the citizens with terror dumb,
Or whispering with white lips, ' The foe—they come—they come.' "

Sister Clara trembled, and hurried more swiftly on her way, as she timidly called up in her imagination the terrible realities which must, and the inconceivable horrors which might be the result of that day's carnage. But she felt that it should be to her, and to those of her vocation, a day of arduous and holy, though dangerous and painful duties, and counted her beads involuntarily as she flitted swiftly on her way, and prayed that she might have the love and courage to fulfill her duties as became a daughter of Christ, whose mission was to carry to the hearts of the unbelieving, the despairing and the needy, the priceless blessings of " faith, hope and charity ;" but most of all charity.

She had started earlier than usual upon her accustomed circuit of morning visits, that she might not be obliged to neglect them for the weightier duties which, with the defence, or possibly the seige or sacking of the city by those who came on under the infamous watchwords of " Beauty and booty," would multiply so infinitely beyond the power of her, and her co-workers to perform.   Before, however, she had reached the doorstep of the unfortunate object of her present visit, the first loud booming of the distant cannon suddenly told her that below the town the fierce contest had already begun.   Scarcely had it struck upon her ears, when within the old, rickety, moss-grown house, upon whose steps she stood, arose a frantic and infuriated shriek, than which its occupant could have sent up none more expressive of hopeless terror if every ball of the distant volley had come rattling down upon the sunken roof, and around the broken, cobwebbed windows of the tottering tenement.

Fearing for the time to go farther, she stood for a moment within the door, expecting, as the loud booming sound increased rather than diminished, to hear, as soon as the demented Iasaacks had sufficiently recovered his strength, to hear the continued raving with which her entrance was usually accompanied, and which by exhausting his strength rendered it safer for her to approach him.   The distant booming cannonade continued, but her patient must have been overwhelmed to silence by his intense fear, for there was no sound. She slammed the front door violently to, but all besides was as still as before.   She repeated the noise, and a sensation of tremulous fear and awe thrilled her at the same unwonted silence.   She hurried along the entry and down the dark and narrow stairs, half expecting every moment to be rudely seized in his insane grasp, for this was the first exception to the usual wild weird manner in which her presence had been acknowledged by her host. But all continued still. No furious grasp rested upon her arm, or threatened to throttle or murder her in fiendish return for her benefactions. She arrived at the door of his apartment. It was ajar—the room was very cold and damp, but there was no fire. There had been fire— the ashes were still wet. Water had been poured upon it, to put it out and save the fuel. She shoved the door widely open, and spoke softly and timidly—

"Iasaacks?"

The coffin lay as usual upon the bed. The lid had been adjusted neatly in its place. Again she called louder and more distinctly—

"Iasaacks—Iasaacks?"

There was no sound. She approached and timidly removed the lid. At first she started back, for the open glazed eye, glaring out from his gaunt, haggard and starved face looked horridly terrible. But in a moment she saw that its lustre had nearly departed. She placed her palm upon his low, retreating brows— they were quite cold. Closing the lids over those fearful, insane orbs, she deprived the face of half its terror. Death, which had long ago rested upon the affections, settled over the moral nature, and darkly clouded the reason, had at last deigned to take possession of the body, which, without a moral, an affectional, or a reasonable nature, it were vain to say, were better out of the grave than in it.

So Sister Clara could not but think as she knelt and offered a prayer for the shattered soul which had just been freed from its tenement. Then rising, she readjusted the lid over the coffin, and took up her basket and crept through the dark passageway up the narrow stair-case, and emerged from the creaking old hall-door once more into the open day. She felt like a weary porter relieved of his burden, as if a duty had been fulfilled ; and the lightness which this consciousness gives under all circumstances, seemed to buoy up her step with a soul-satisfying joy, which went far to dispel the sadness of the scene she had just witnessed. But the roar of the distant cannon hurried her away to new and more arduous labors.

How different was her mission from that of nearly all of the thousands who had earlier on that morning hastened to the same eventful scene. They, strong in the flush of life, health and manly strength, had hurried there to wound, to slay, to blast and curse their fellow men. She, weak in all these things, and clad only in the armor of faith and charity, hastened thither, to bind up, and heal, to pour oil into their bleeding wounds, and give consolation to their dying souls.

When she arrived upon the field, the contest was just over. Not ill pleased to learn, but rendering fervent gratitude to heaven that the enemies of her country had been driven back in defeat, she set herself immediately to inquiring for those to whom she might be of service.

" You had better go on the 'tother side of Jackson's cotton if you want business in that line," replied a soldier, proudly, of whom she had inquired where the wounded and dying had been carried. " I don't think there's anybody hurt among us. I arn't heerd nobody complain, except the brave fellows that went over there to try and help our enemies wounded, and act'ly got shot at by them they tried to help for their pains. But over there I think you'll find a few," he continued, pointing beyond the entrenchments at the wide plain piled for a quarter of a mile with the slain and curs- ing, writhing and yelling wounded, indicating how determined and firm had been the advance of the vete- rans who had fought under Wellington on the Penin- sula, and how ruthlessly they had been mowed down and defeated by the militia ploughmen of Tennessee.

" Were there really no wounded among our party ?" questioned Sister Clara eagerly.

" Perhaps there might have been a few. They say
12*

there were half a dozen or so," said the soldier, trying to assume the indifference of a veteran, while a tear stood in his eye. "Noble fellows ! 'specially that infernal ' Conrad' and his crew from Barrataria. They fought in the very hottest of it, when the enemy had very nearly carried the works, and would have done so but for those d—— piratical cutlasses which, when it came to close quarters, fiddled away upon their enemies' throats until they made them sing a most terrible tune. I think you'll find them at the head-quarters of the General," said the soldier, or rather the boy, for he could not have passed eighteen, pointing at the same time to a large flag-tent, around which many soldiers and curious citizens had already gathered. From the random remarks dropped from the persons who formed the crowd, as she hurried through it, which she easily did, where all quickly made way for her in double reverence for her sex and sacred habit, she rejoiced to learn that there were among the Americans but " eight killed and thirteen wounded."

She found ready admission to the tent, upon entering which, her attention was immediately withdrawn from every other group to one, the figures in which she recognized.

There, recumbent upon a pallet of military cloaks, which had been laid down to receive him, and his head supported by a woman, who bent fondly and tenderly over him, lay the wounded and bleeding form of Conrad Defoe. His proud, handsome features were livid with the paleness of death, and a languid stupor was settling over his lately piercing and passionate eye. A gashed arm, at which his angry eye flashed in impatient resentment, seemed to fill every moment with unutterable pangs. But beneath that arm, from a wound in his side breast, the gushing of the red arterial gore was painlessly, but rapidly bearing away his life. Oh, between the late terrible "Conrad," as he rushed into the melee of battle, fierce, impetuous, and powerful, striking down the enemies of his country with his own strong arm and trusty sabre, as he only could who combined the bravery and skill of one who had long fought in a bad cause, with the zeal of one who was then fighting in a good one ; and that same Conrad, as he now, with clotted locks, and pallid hue, and deathly languor, glared restlessly, feebly, and feverishly around him—what a contrast ! Languidly, ever and anon, he parts his heavy lids with difficulty, and rolls his fading orbs around, as if expecting the appearance of some person, and whispers, huskily—

"Annette, is he coming yet ?"

Just now a tall, old man, with a piercing gray eye and commanding, soldierly bearing, steps quickly to the side of the wounded Conrad, and bending low over him, says—

"Courage, comrade—you may yet hope."

"Ah, is it you, commander ?" smiled the dying one, over whose dark and troubled features a ray of sunlight seemed to steal, as he felt his general's hand. "No, there is no hope for me. I am sinking," he cried, his hands clasped in anguish, "into a fearful, a terrible grave. But no more of that. You know me. I am Conrad Defoe. My brother, in prison, has been mistaken for me. He is innocent. You will see that injustice is no longer done him ?"

"I will," was the response, in clear, deep tones, which satisfied the soldier's heart.

"One word more. This woman, Annette, is my wife. She has not a friend. I commend her to you."

"Oh, Sister Clara," said Annette, in tears, as the former now knelt down beside her, "you have sought me long, and at last you have found me. But tell me, quick—is my father living ?"

Sister Clara shook her head negatively. For a moment Annette buried her hand in her bosom. As she withdrew it, her bosom and hand both were stained with crimson. Beckoning to the Sister to support the head of Conrad in her stead, she moved to his side, and resting one arm upon the ground, and passing the other tenderly around him, she gazed in longing affection into his eye. From her bosom the rich red stream of life was gushing forth and mingling with his own.

" No, husband ; commend me to none. There is none for whom I should live—no, not one. Have I not said that I will die with thee ? See here," she said, withdrawing the folds of her dress from the fatal wound which her own hand had just inflicted, " I have struck home."

As she said this, her head sunk with weakness, lower and lower, over him, till her breast rested upon his own, and their life-blood mingled in a common stream. She had indeed struck home. The trembling motion of her lips—the heaving and falling of her bosom, soon ceased, and she grew cold in his embrace. A smile wreathed his lips at this last needless evidence of a too fatal constancy, which hung upon them for hours. At last his smile also grew cold, and stark, and stiff, in the chill embrace of death ; and he, too, slept.

> " He left a corsair's name to other times,
> Linked with one virtue and a thousand crimes."

CHAPTER XXXI.

THE CAPTIVE.

" Imputed madness, prisoned solitude,
  And the mind's canker in its savage mood,
When the impatient thirst of light and air
Parches the heart ; and the abhorred grate,
Marring the sunbeams with its hideous shade,
Works through the throbbing eye-ball to the brain,
With a hot sense of heaviness and pain ;
And bare, at once, Captivity displayed,
  Stands scoffing through the never-opened gate,
Which nothing through its bars admits save day,
And tasteless food which I have eat alone,
Till its unsocial bitterness is gone ;
And I can banquet like a beast of prey,
Sullen and lonely, crouching in the cave,
Which is my lair, and—it may be—my grave."
BYRON'S LAMENT OF TASSO.

THE next morning's sun had hardly risen upon the
field of battle. Its faint rays came peering sadly into
the dungeon of Walter, who, slowly recovering from
his wounds, had begun with more painful weariness
to feel the tedium of his solitary cell. What were
his thoughts as he lay stretched upon his straw couch,
or rising, stared around upon his prison walls. His
own prospect, notwithstanding his innocence, was

gloomy. The anomalous and deceptive circumstances under which he was captured, and the strong likeness he bore to Conrad Defoe, insomuch that the few who knew the latter almost unanimously agreed in identifying him as the man, seemed to leave him no room for doubt that an ignominious death—the death of a common enemy of mankind—awaited him.

And how did *she* regard him—the pure, amiable, and high-souled Julia? Was he mentioned only upon her lips as an outlaw and a wretch? The thought distracted him.

Through the visits of the kind Sister Clara, whose brain was almost kindled into frenzy by the wrongs inflicted upon her daughter, he had learned that Julia was now in a slave pen, awaiting a sale at public auction.

Yes, before him, upon his prison walls, was posted the notice of sale—a handbill which Sister Clara had brought to him. Through the livelong night, though he could not see it, his eyes had been turned towards it, with the stare of approaching insanity ; but as morning dawned, he was enabled once more to read its fearful characters :

FOR SALE AT AUCTION,

On Jan. 29th inst., at 10, A. M.,

WITHOUT RESERVE,

THE BEAUTIFUL AND NEARLY

WHITE SLAVE JULIA!

Aged 19—highly educated, refined and pious—suitable for Governess or Companion—now on exhibition. Call and see her at the pen of J. SWINGLER.

Fixedly and vacantly the sick, wounded, and half-demented lover gazed upon the terrible announcement, in utter and powerless despair. The sun was now far up in the horizon, and the mind of Walter, in a clairvoyant dream, was with his mistress in her slave pen. The hour had nearly arrived. Even now he saw them entering to lead her away to the sale. The bell upon the tower had struck nine.

"Why do these prison walls enclose me? Burst asunder—open for me!" shrieked Walter, wildly raving. But still the dead stones shut him in. "I tell you, burst asunder! In the name of innocence, of justice, and of God, fly apart, ye doors!" raved the lunatic, insanely.

But the iron doors moved not.

He rose, with the calm confidence of the maniac, whose perverted and disordered fancy seems to subject everything to his will, and shouted—

"Again, and for the last time, I command, fly back, ye bolts—open, ye bars !"

This time the bolt did fly back, the strong door opened, and the bailiff, followed by no less remarkable a couple than the ubiquitous Sister Clara and the lengthy Snaacks, appeared.

"My son, my son—God be praised, you are free !" shrieked Sister Clara, rushing into his arms, without waiting for the slow jailor to read the warrant he held in his hands.

"Free !" shouted Walter, "ha ! ha ! ha !" And he laughed in his hysteric madness, with a maniac laugh that chilled the Sister to the very soul.

"And I have the honor," said Snaacks, with more than his usual celerity of speech, "to deliver to you the title papers of the late Moses Iasaacks, a respected client of mine, whose estate, by his death, having descended to his daughter, the wife of your late brother, and both your brother and his wife having died, has passed to you as their sole heir at law. The amount, sir, of your wealth, including the Preston estate, which, by the recent foreclosure of a mortgage thereon, has just been added thereto, is almost incalculable, and I only trust that his long experience in managing the estate, will induce you to retain as your attorney the past incumbent of that responsible position, your obedient servant, Mr. Snaacks. Full returns shall be made quarterly, as heretofore, and moneys invested on good security——"

How long Mr. Snaacks would have protracted his speech, we would not pretend to say, had not Walter, over whose dim returning intellect some faint realization of his true circumstances was slowly stealing, been aroused and fully restored to his scattered senses, as the clock struck ten.

"Away, away!" he cried, "to the slave pen—to the rescue!"

But the little strength which his wounds and sickness had left him, failed him in the intensity of his excitement; and sinking inanimate into their arms, they bore him out of the jail and along the street, in the direction he had indicated. The cool air of the street fanned and refreshed him, and he was in a few moments able to rise and accompany them.

Let us hasten there in time to precede by a few moments his arrival.

CHAPTER XXXII.

SOULS AT AUCTION.

" Without, surrounded by a motley crowd,
The shrewd-eyed salesman, garrulous and loud ;
A squire or colonel in his pride of place,
Known at free fights, the caucus, and the race,
Prompt to proclaim his honor without blot,
*　　*　　*　　*　　*　　*
Yet never scrupling, with a filthy jest,
To sell the infant from its mother's breast—
Break through all ties of wedlock, home, and kin,
Yield shrinking girlhood up to gray-beard sin ;
Sell all the virtues with his human stock—
The Christian graces on his auction block ;
And coolly count on shrewdest bargains driven,
In hearts regenerate, and in souls forgiven."

WHITTIER.

" 'BISNESS is bisness'—that's my motto, an' I b'leeve it's a good one," shouted the little squat-shouldered, low-visaged, red-haired Mr. Swingler, from his throne on the elevated auction-block in the centre of the yard. "And when it's done, it's done, gentlemen—them's my conwictions ; an' what can a hon'ble man do better as follerin' his conwictions ?

" Now, gentlemen, I've got a few common niggers,

compar'tively speakin' that is, an' I'll put 'em on the block ; and the thing you've mostly come for will be the next thing on the board."

This speech was addressed to a mixed crowd, made up of a few inland planters, just come in town to buy a stock of hands, a large sprinkling of gamblers, black-legs and fancy men, several stray negro children and dirty whites, and some nondescript hangers-on, to whom it would be difficult to assign any description or occupation.

" Bring in No. One," shouted Swingler.

"Gemmen, here's No. One—as fine a little nigger as you ever owned. Five years old, an' not a scar on him ; not a bruise. If that don't show him a good disposition, I'd like to know what would. Goin', gemmen ; anything to ·start the bid. What do I hear ? Do I hear fifty dollars ? Do I hear fifty ?"

As nobody seemed disposed to inform him whether he heard fifty or not, Mr. Swingler concluded he had not, and so bawled—

"Away· with the d——d nigger ! Bring on No. Two."

No. Two was a young mulatto, of unmistakably strong passions and good intellect. He mounted the block with a defiant air of superiority, rather than with the abject submission of a slave ; and as he looked around upon the hundred or more persons, either of whom might within a minute become his owner, his expression was one which would strike every experienced purchaser as that of a man sullen and hard to manage.

" No. Two is now up," said Swingler.

No. Two, however, now held his head, and seemed decidedly down.

" What do you say for him ? A smart nigger. Look at the scars. Been well broke in, you see. Walk up and examine his teeth, gemmen."

Here a gentleman walked up, and putting his thumbs into the negro's mouth, made a thorough and apparently satisfactory examination of his teeth.

" Perfectly sound. Going, going, going ! What do you say for him ?"

But no bids were heard, and Mr. Swingler ordered No. Two back, with the further suggestion—

" Give the d——d nigger fifteen lashes ; it will put him into a smile. Who the hell's going to buy such a d——d sulky devil ! I'll show him a thing or two. Now, gentlemen, we'll have a little the nicest girl that ever went to market. I have sold such things afore in my time, but I tell you—— Boys, bring out No. Three. No, not often, gentlemen, you can buy such property as No. Three."

Disdaining the touch of the attendants who would have led her forth, with eyes not suffused with tears, but flashing with suppressed rage, Julia advanced with a firm, elastic step, and after upraising her dark orbs for a few moments, as if in prayer, to heaven, for support through this last and most degrading ordeal, she turned and faced the curious and disgusting gaze of the wondering audience, with a dignity not unlike that with which a brave European princess, wrecked among savages, would have looked around at her captors.

"Here, gentlemen, is No. Three," said Swingler, mounting by her side ; and taking her by the hand, he would have held it up after his manner with female slaves, as a tradesman would exhibit his stuffs.

"Hands off, low man !" shrieked Julia, starting suddenly from him, and bending her eagle eye for a moment upon him, with a fierceness before which he quailed. "Hands off, vile monster, I repeat."

"Yer see, gentlemen," said Swingler, swallowing, with an ill grace, his anger, "yer see she's a gal of pluck. She ain't tamed yet. But any o' yer as wants a putty governess——"

"Silence, dog ! be silent, I tell you," screamed No. Three, with a fury that cowed him. Sell me, work me, lash me to your heart's content, if you choose, but *dare* not to insult me !"

Swingler's finger twitched nervously around the

handle of a whip which he held in his hands. Could he endure such impudence?

"Now, you know," said Swingler, turning appealingly to the bystanders, "no man will take more from a white man than I will, but, by G——, no man will take less from a nigger."

But some of the spectators were merciful, and cried out—

"Set her up—we're ready to bid—never mind the speech if the gal's squirmish!"

Swingler complied.

"Goin'—goin'—goin'. Gentlemen, start the bid bold, for I don't let her go at no small price. By G——, I want to thrash her liver out on her afore she leaves Joe Swingler's pen. So you bid high or she won't go at this sale. Goin', goin'—what do I hear? Start it at five hundred."

Four hundred and fifty dollars then, a high price, was bid.

"Four fifty—five hundred is bid—five—five—five fifty. She can't possibly sell for less than one thousand, gentlemen. Walk up an' look at her. Don't be afeared, gemmen, if she is shy. Feel of her, gentlemen."

In compliance with this request, a flashly dressed young man, with a dissipated *blazè* air, sauntered up, and was about to place his hand upon her shoulder.

" Away with you—wretch among wretches," shrieked the proud girl.

This insult to a customer was more than Swingler
could bear.

" Wretches, eh ! Wretches, eh ! I'll show you
who are wretches. Give me my whip. Here, John,
Bill, Sam, hold the white skinned wench, while I lash
her."

Three stout negroes advanced, but respectfully hesi-
tated to lay hands upon her, for ignorance, however
deep, still recognizes and respects the true lady with
politeness, which depravity, however cultivated, fails
in the attempt to dissemble. Julia sunk upon her
knees and looked around upon the pitiless visages of
the slave-buyers with an expression of despair which
might have softened the stoniest heart, and piteously
shrieked as she saw the long-lash preparing to descend
upon her.

" Oh, God, help me."

" God help you, you strumpet !" roared Swingler.
God d—— your half-white soul. I tell you once more,
call on *me* for help. This 'ere slave-pen I'm lord and
master of. God Almighty ain't known around
these——"

Ere he had finished the sentence, he lay sprawling
upon the earth by a furious blow from the hand of
Walter Defoe, who that moment sprang through the

crowd, and summoning all his strength, in spite of the effects of his recent wounds and sickness, felled the blaspheming fiend, and was now bending over the fainting form of Julia, who only whispered—

"Dear, dear Walter, I felt that you were coming to save me. Oh, these awful horrors. Take—me—away," and sunk exhausted into his embrace.

"By what authority is all this?" demanded Swingler, rising.

"Mr. Snaacks," said he, addressing that gentleman, who had now come up, "Do you know anything about this houtaloo? The gal's Mr. Preston's, and I have a power of attorney from him to sell her."

"A mistake," replied Snaacks, "this piece of property was of course included in the general mortgage given upon all his goods and chattels to Mr. Iasaacks, my client, of whom this young man is the heir-at-law. The property not yet having passed into the hands of any innocent purchaser, he has the undoubted right to foreclose, which you see he has done."

"I don't believe a word of it, and I demand damages any way for the crack on my head," growled Swingler.

"If you will prove that your head is a thing capable of being damaged, or in any way made worse than it is, we will pay you," replied Snaacks, with that contempt with which the slave-trader is everywhere treated by the slave-owner. "In the mean time we will convey this young lady to a carriage."

Swingler set down upon his auction block and muttered gloomily as they drove off, "A d——n good job spoiled!"

CHAPTER XXXIII.

CONCLUSION.

> " I saw two clouds at morning,
>   Tinged with the rising sun ;
> And in the dawn they floated on,
>   And mingled into one :
> I thought that morning cloud was blest,
> It moved so sweetly to the West."   BRAINARD.

A MONTH had swiftly glided away, and evening's soft shadows again stole down upon Lindenhall, whose usual silence was to-night exchanged for merry voices, music, dancing, and revelry.

From near and far, old and young men and maidens, of the hospitable planters of Louisiana, had come to the marriage of the wealthy young master of Linden-hall with the lovely girl whose history, especially now that she was restored to her true position, touched a responsive chord in the hearts of all. Lingering emotions of sadness there were, indeed, as Julia stepped through the halls familiar to her childhood, and saw nothing of the two forms in childhood so dear to her. Her gentle sister Ada she could not forget ; and as she went to the front windows. and looked out upon the river at the spot where, as Sister Clara had learned from the dying confession of Conrad, her sister had taken her last look at the home of her infancy and of the world, her eyes were suffused with tears.

"Do not weep, my daughter," said Sister Clara, whom her child's experience had induced to dissolve her connection with the Sisters—"do not weep, for this is your wedding day, and I had thought you were very happy."

"Poor, poor sister Ada !" murmured Julia, and her tears flowed afresh,

But spite of this tinge of sadness, Julia felt, as the last words of the ceremony fell from the lips of the good Father Reilly, and she leaned upon the arm of her husband, that so far as the past would permit, the cup of the present was full of deep, blissful joy.

There was joy, too, among the lowly. Not only the whole force of the Preston plantation, but also several scores of negroes—the former property of the demented Jew—had assembled down at the quarters, some of them gaily dressed ; hotel waiters and barbers, ashamed to be seen in company with field negroes ; some mechanics and book-keepers, with their intelligent countenances and light mulatto wives and children, were mingled with low, slatternly clodhoppers and field hands, who felt ill at ease in the new garments in which they had gaudily decked themselves for the occasion. Many of them had heretofore been let to various employers at a stipulated price, and allowed to retain a certain portion of the price as their own, with which, by long and patient diligence and economy, they had nearly saved enough to buy their liberty. But now what was their joy, for their new master had been among them, and to those who had nearly accomplished the work of purchasing their liberty, he had remitted the balance, and freed not only themselves, but their aged parents and wives and children. Upon those who, heretofore less apt, industrious or prudent, had not been educated to thriftiness, Walter had concluded to impose certain easy terms as the price of their freedom, which would at the same time fit them better for the competition with the always free and skilled laborer of the North, upon which they would enter, and would make them feel a greater degree of pride in the liberty which they had earned ; for he felt that to free some of them immediately, with those habits of thoughtlessness, laziness, and improvidence, which the system of slavery had left them with, would be a boon as dangerous as to right a patient who had been sent to an infected hospital, when he had no disease, by freeing him after the disease was upon him. Tears of gratitude were in every eye. A third of the fortune which Walter had inherited, had nw assembled with its free papers in its hands, and so much of his riches would soon take wings and fly away ; but as his benevolent heart went out to them in freedom, he thanked God, who had thus given him the means of bringing joy to the hearts of the lowly.   No wealth could have so rewarded him, or have made his heart leap with such pure, un-alloyed joy, as when, before the festivities were over, and while the aristocratic, though social sons and daughters of wealth were joined in the merry dance, a deputation, in the person of the delighted "Alexander," waited upon him with a request from "de colored ladies and gemmen" outside, that they might be permitted to serenade them.   Good naturedly granting their request, the company listened to the following strain, sung in that simple, yet touching style of melody of which the African is the inimitable originator :

THE SLAVES' SERENADE.

White folks—pleas hear de darkies' song,
  Before you go away ;
We want to tell—it won't take long,
  How glad we are to-day.

    Chorus—Ring—ring—de banjo—Ole Massa gone,
      De new one set us free,
      Roar wid de fiddle—bang de bone,
      Ho! yah! how glad we be !

De poor ole slave—his heart am joy,
  Dough tears am in his eye—
For free is he, his wife an' boy;
  How can dat tear be dry!
      Chorus—Ring—ring—de banjo, &c.

He dance all day, he dance all night,
  Likewise de cage-bird sing,
But bress de han' dat free him quite,
  And gib de cage-bird wing.
      Chorus—Ring—ring—de banjo, &c.

We know we are poor slaves by law
  But mercy set us free,
An' He will bress you from whom a'
  Can only ask mercy.
      Chorus—Ring—ring—de banjo, &c.

Good-bye—good-bye, our massa dear,
  Our missus, too, good-bye ;—
We meet whar slave shed neber tear,
  Whar massa neber sigh.
      Chorus—An' dar we'll sing, ole massa gone,
        New one set us free,
        And play de harp an' de soft trombone,
        How happy dar we be!

Just as the last strain of the melody, which was sung and played in a truly touching if not artistic style, died away, the sharp crack of fire-arms was heard immediately under the windows of the mansion —a heavy falling and a groan, as of one wounded, followed. The company started—the ladies shrieked, and gentlemen seizing lights, rushed in the direction of the fearful sound.

There, with a discharged pistol in his right hand,

another having just fallen from the left—prostrate upon the sward, over which his blood and brains were scattered, lay the former proprietor of Lindenhall, Butler Preston. After having maintained the strict-est silence and concealment for the past month, stung by remorse, overwhelmed by rage, shame and chargin, having no motive to survive his irrecoverable disgrace, he had returned to the scene of the wealth he had abused and the opportunities for good which he had prostituted to evil—to blow out his brains.

Many years have glided serenely and happily away since then. With the immense fortune placed at his disposal, but which has considerably diminished in the advancement of his philanthropic schemes, Walter Defoe has been constant to the lofty dream of usefulness which cheered and ennobled the struggles of his youth. Not unmindful of that time when all he held most sacred upon earth, stood with uplifted hands and tearful eyes, in the presence of her buyers—her humanity degraded—her immortality denied—her every right infamously and brutally trampled upon—owned as a chattel and therefore disowned as a child—he did not hesitate for a long time boldly and publicly to oppose the institution which had legalized the outrage, and privately to labor to mitigate its evils in such special and peculiar instances as came under his knowledge. For a while the influence of his immense fortune, his talents, tact and many amiable social qualities, enabled him to pursue this course comparatively without molestation. During this season of privileged opportunity, he endeavored to sow the seeds of a loftier and more honorable feeling among masters generally, by which they should look upon themselves not merely as the owners, but also as the beneficent guardians of their slaves, and as such bound to educate them so far as their capacity would admit, and elevate and christianize them—looking upon the slaves not merely as cattle to be worked in this world, but as immortal souls to be prepared for the next.

Particularly urgent was he for the repeal or modification of those laws which prohibit the education of slaves under penalties more frightful than those visited upon many flagrant felonies, which place obstacles in the way of emancipation, and which give the owner such an unlimited sway over the life and limbs as well as the liberty of the slave. To encourage a respect also for the unity of families, to prevent the eternal and bittes separations of husbands and wives, parents and children, brothers and sisters, and to maintain the inviolability of the laws of morality in the intercourse of the master and slave, were also among his enthusiastic but ill-requited labors. His efforts in this behalf were principally useful, however, in making him acquainted with those individual instances of special injustice, which his ample means were ever ready to relieve.

Many honest hearts, beating beneath tawny skins, far away under his own northern sky, offered up daily prayers of gratitude for deliverance from bondage, and called down blessings upon him as their deliverer.

The fear of diminishing his estate, never, in a solitary instance, deterred him from giving liberty to whomsoever he could. Whether they were "sufficiently developed to be entitled to their freedom," was in his view a miserable interrogatory which he did not ask. The sacred charter of American liberty ceased not to thunder in his ear—"ALL MEN ARE CREATED EQUAL, and are endowed by their Creator with certain inalienable rights, among which are life, liberty, and the pursuit of happiness." With this gospel before him, he could but preach freedom to all, not merely in his words and pretensions, which is cheaply and easily done; but more expensively also by his acts.

But there are two classes of people to whom the common sense or prevailing opinions and common laws of mankind are equally opposed, viz., the extremely bad and the extremely good. As one of the latter, he was proscribed by the American despot, public opinion. When much of his fortune had faded away in the industry of his philanthropic efforts, and the influence which his wealth at first gave him was somewhat diminished, he was accused as an agitator and incendiary.

Incendiary ! Look, gentle reader, who hast not yet learned to despise words and hold fast only to their meaning, over the entire field of human history, and learn how often that word is applied to the pioneer of light and liberty and truth, because he burns down the thorny thickets of error, darkness and slavery, that God's green harvest may wave in their place !

To him the alternative was presented of discontinuing his philanthropic labors, of leaving the district in which he had resided, or of remaining and continuing those labors at his peril. His resolution was immediately taken. Sell out, and transfer those slaves, to whose approaching emancipation he looked forward as a parent looks forward to the majority of his child ! No. Permit them to pass into the hands of other owners, who would entail endless bondage upon their posterity, he could not. Free them he must. He spake and they were free.

Deprived thus of what was found, after paying his debts, to be nearly the whole of the estate, he devoted the remainder to the pious fulfillment of imperative obligations of gratitude, by investing it for the benefit of Sister Clara and of the kind old Quakeress of his

infancy. Once more, therefore, cheered and encouraged by the love of Julia, he now, in the prime
of manhood, returned to the North with as little
means as those with which he had left it, and entered
with the labor of his own hands and head upon the
pursuit not merely of fortune but of usefulness.
Could he fail ? Never !

After a long career of noble success, the merchant
prince has retired from the excitement of his counting-
house in the metropolis, to his beautiful villa upon tho
banks of the Hudson.   We cannot describe it to you,
but, gentle reader, if you will call upon us on some
one of those beautiful October days, when a sail in a
steamer or yacht over the bosom of that noble river
is so delightful, when the woods that conceal its romantic shores, are clothed in their autumnal richness
and glory, and the air is balmy and delicious, we will
point it out to you.

There, when we last saw him, he sat upon a rustic
seat, beneath the branches of a weeping willow, that
stands down by the water's edge, in front of his mansion, which resembles Lindenhall, after which it is
named, as much as possible in its architectural
style.   There also are fac-similes of the green lawn,
the groves of cypress, the branching willow, and the
rustic couch beneath, upon which Walter and Julia
sat on a certain eventful evening.   And there too in

that rustic couch now sat the ripe, hale Walter, whose hair is beginning to be silvered, and his still handsome wife, her long dark hair as jetty, her complexion as brunette, her lips as rich and red and almost as tempting, and her large lustrous black eyes, full as bright, fiery and flashing as ever.

In rural arm-chairs, one upon either side of the rustic seat above mentioned, sat two old ladies with wrinkled countenances, whose benevolent expression made them lovely. One of them was dressed with the scrupulous neatness, precision and plainness of a Quakeress. The other is Sister Clara. She had just removed her spectacles to wipe from her eyes a tear, which had involuntarily moistened them, for Mr. Defoe had just finished perusing the manuscript of a book in which a young friend had set forth the history of the romantic vicissitudes of a portion of the life of Julia and himself.

A bright looking little girl (their youngest) in whom we scarcely know whether more closely to trace the features of Walter or of Julia, was standing beside his knee.

" Is that all, papa ?" she lisped, looking up to him sweetly as the volume closed.

" That is all."

" Well, do tell us what became of Sandy."

" I think you will find him at the house."

"What ! old uncle Sandy, who is so good-natured and fat, and whose wool is so white ? Is he the same ? Sure enough, I knew he'd always been with you. Why, how very old he is, isn't he ? Wouldn't it be funny to see him jump out of a second story window now though ?" exclaimed the little girl, clapping her hands at the idea.

"And what became of good old Betsey, and aunt Tanzey, and old Tim ?"

"They did not wish their freedom, but lived and died with us. They died long ago."

"Oh, yes," exclaimed the little one, "as the song says, they

"Died long ago—long ago,"

and I suppose she continued singing—

"They had no wool on de top o' der heads,
De place whar de wool ought to grow."

"But now, papa," she whispered, throwing her little arms around his neck and kissing him, "Tell me, is that all true, or is it a novel ?"

"Substantially true, child," replied Mr. Defoe.

THE END.

www.ingramcontent.com/pod-product-compliance
Lightning Source LLC
Chambersburg PA
CBHW020940120726
47905CB00008B/2606